Explicit Erotic Sex Stories

The best sex you have ever read, the perfect stories to express your deepest desires and apply them with your partner

Organizer (Gangbangs)

Tonya will organize anything...anything at all.

Ian Lorelle was thirty-five years old when he left Shana, his wife of nine years. It was all he could do to keep his sanity. Toward the end, she stopped trying to hide the fact she was cheating on him. She would come home late with wine on her breath and sperm in her hair, or sometimes vice-versa. The laundry hamper even took on the smell of cheap cologne.

Oddly enough, he wouldn't have minded her being with other guys if she'd been honest. They had talked about partner sharing with a small group of folks they knew were into it. On one occasion, they went so far as to visit one of those couples to see if chatting might lead to something more risqué. Shana quipped and giggled about it over a glass of wine, but she got cold feet when their hostess began unbuttoning Ian's shirt.

That incident proved ironic to Ian a month later when he came home from work early. As usual, he galloped up the stairs to their second floor apartment. As he opened the door, he heard a man let out a protracted moan. Bolting into the living room, he found their upstairs neighbor still buttoning his pants as Shana hastily wiped her chin on her sleeve.

After that, it was a short, steep, downhill slide to separation. Ian floundered for a week, thinking Shana may show remorse, but she responded by again stepping out and flaunting her iniquity.

When he came home to find her legs wrapped around a guy she worked with, he packed a suitcase and checked into an efficiency apartment.

One Friday after work, he met his old friend, Cliff Gray to grab a quick beer and lament his woes. "I'm not going back to her," he insisted as they sat at a table. "I don't need the bullshit."

"Atta boy," boasted Cliff. "And have a little fun before you look to settle down again. You're still young. Enjoy your freedom."

"Easier said than done," complained Ian. "I set up a profile on an online—"

"Don't bother," interrupted Cliff. "You'll waste your time getting charged up over someone who isn't who they say they are." He took a swig from his mug and leaned his elbows on the table. "You want a no-worries guarantee to get laid?"

"Yeah, but I don't want my dick to fall off."

"Join Mingling Singles, bro."

"Are you kidding? That's full of mothers looking for a new daddy for their kid."

"Maybe, but it's a meat market. How do ya' think they try to hook a new papa, anyway? Just don't propose to anyone."

"You're shittin' me."

"I shit you not. I went there when I divorced Crystal. Wet my noodle almost every week."

"And you wound up with Deanne."

"But not until I made the rounds, partner. By the time I met Deanne, I was worried my balls would shrivel. Besides she's a helluva good girlfriend. I don't need to make the rounds anymore."

"Why not? Is she that good?"

"Something like that. I'll tell you all about it some time." He finished his beer and stood, grabbing his jacket. "Gotta go," he concluded. "Just show up at the Elks Lodge tomorrow. They meet every Saturday at seven."

Cliff's call was on the money. The very first night, Ian wound up bouncing his belly off a chubby but cute set of butt-cheeks. The middle-age mom insisted he go bareback and was more than happy to let him come in her. She sucked him back to size and swallowed his second batch, then begged him to top her off with another load. What's more, she stroked his ego back into shape by washing his balls in a few gushes of girlie reward.

On the down side, she did it all in a whisper. With her two kids sleeping in the room across the hall, she insisted he stay quiet as well. Grasping her love-handles, Ian pursed his lips and puffed his cheeks as he pressed his thighs against the backs of hers, jetting his last salvoes of the evening into a viscous pool inside her. It was by far the best sex he'd had in years, albeit a silent event.

As he retreated from her seed-laden channel, a shrill cry came from across the hall, followed by, "Mommy!"

With a bead of cum still dripping from her crevice, she pushed her arms into a robe and whispered, "I'll try to get my parents to watch them this weekend."

Ian was the conscientious type. He hoped she would eventually find Mr. Right, but it wasn't going to be him. He said hello to her at the next meeting, but left with a classy businesswoman named Sandra, who he recognized as the loan officer at the local bank.

Sandra was just as quick to get started, but something was wrong from the start. She made him park down the street, and insisted they have their soirée on an old sofa in the basement. Clearly, her ex wasn't as good with their separation as she claimed. Ian expected him to be at the door at any minute, bringing their eleven-year-old son back early.

Afterward, Sandra promised things would smooth out soon. She gave great head and squealed in pleasure as she swallowed his load. Ian lost track of how many times he came in her, but his balls ached as he drove home. She smiled and waved the next few times he went to the bank, but Ian pretended not to see her.

By week three, Ian was on a roll. Buried deep in unfamiliar genealogy, he sprayed the velvety inners of a middle-age redhead with spurts of viscous warmth. His balls tingled in blissful pangs as he pumped his semen into her thin frame. She gave a needy coo into the mattress as his bursts faded off to bumps. Much like week-one, the antics came to an end with a knock on the door. Unlike week-one, the knock wasn't from a child, but rather a crying ex-husband.

He went to Mingling Singles for several more weeks, only going home alone a few times, but a pattern was unfolding. The walls were closing in. Sooner or later, he would have to choose a partner and "graduate" like Cliff did, or his prospects would dry up and he would be thrown to the cougars prowling the back tables. Deep down, he had hoped to find a gal with a more open mind toward sexuality, maybe one who would give partner-sharing a try. Apparently, he wouldn't find her at Mingling Singles.

Or so he thought. Each time he went, he couldn't help but notice one particular gal in her early thirties. Although she was at Mingling Singles every Saturday night, she seldom spoke to anyone. She didn't sit at any of the tables during hors d'oeuvres, or mingle afterward. Ian figured she organized the events, since she set up the food table and always hung around to clean up the hall. But she was no wallflower, either. Her walk had a dainty, playful purpose and on the few occasions he heard her laugh, she all but sang.

At first, her appearance struck him as ordinary. She had no particular quality that caught the eye with a single glance. But seeing her time and again, he found her unique combination of features manifested into a precious example of femininity. She stood a thin but shapely five-foot-six. Her long, full hair struck two shades of blonde—golden and sandy layers that framed deep blue eyes.

She usually dressed rather plainly in jeans or black yoga pants, a simple blouse, and moccasins or flat shoes. Only toward the end of each night would she take off her denim jacket to show her slender arms. As Ian watched her each week, he sensed an esoteric, easy-going quality in the air around her, even before he ever spoke to her.

When he did, he wound up plenty confused. She was wiping down a tablecloth as he approached.

"Would you like some help?" he asked.

"Does it come with a price?" she queried without looking up.

"Just a name," he replied, folding the tablecloth as she wiped another. "I was hoping you'd volunteer the rest. I'm—"

"Ian," she interrupted. "I pay attention."

"What have you noticed about me?"

"For starters," she replied, hauling a table like a puny dockworker, "You've been sampling the most vulnerable girls."

"I didn't mean any harm. I was just—"

"Dipping your worm in a kettle of fish," she called back, carrying a bowl of salad into the kitchen.

"You can't blame me for being successful," he bargained, calling through the doorway to her.

"I don't blame you," she sang, strutting out and handing him a push-broom.

"So you'll tell me your name?"

"Nope."

"That's it? No explanation?"

"I don't think you'd care for the company I keep," she snipped.

"Are you a lesbian?"

She huffed and rolled her eyes. "Why?" she asked, looking up. "Why do they always ask that?"

"Maybe because you're being aloof," he suggested.

"Aloof? I've never been accused of that before."

"Not that you've heard. If you shut people down that fast, you're likely to miss a lot. All I asked for was your name."

11

"It's Tonya Forsythe. Satisfied?"

"Nope. Now I want you to come out for coffee, Tonya Forsythe."

"Is that all?" she asked sarcastically.

"Would you believe me if I said it was?"

Ten minutes later, they sat sipping coffee at a donut shop across the street from the rental hall. "Honestly," offered Ian, "I asked you for a different reason than...you know..."

"All the others?" she asked, sipping her coffee.

"You think I'm a dog, huh?"

"Mm-hmm," she replied with a nod.

"Then why'd you come?"

"Something you touched on."

"Well, I doubt you're a lesbian."

"Bi."

"That doesn't bother me."

"I wouldn't care if it did."

"So what'd I touch on?"

"Not telling, but I'll let you know if you touch on it again."

"I'm only asking—"

"I know what you're asking for," she offered in a playful intonation, standing to leave.

"Am I being too bold?" he asked, standing and reaching her denim coat off the hook.

"You're bold," she replied. "But not too bold." She looked him up and down, standing only to his chin. Raising her gaze to meet his, she broke a cute smile over her glossed lips. "How open-minded are you?" she asked.

"Open enough to not care if you're bi."

"Childs' play," she purred. "Follow me in your car. We'll see how bold you are."

And follow he did—under the highway and past the waterfront, then over the bridge to the town of Wellsburgh, where Tonya pulled into the driveway of a stately home. Ian pulled in behind her and scurried over to her car. "Nice house," he offered, noticing the dozen or so cars parked on the side lawn.

"I've only been here a few times," she replied as he followed her up the steps. Ringing the bell, she turned to face him and with a spearing glance of her blue eyes warned, "Last chance."

"You're trying to scare me off."

"For your own good," she retorted as the latch clicked. The door swung open to reveal a pretty, middle-age brunette in a black dress hemmed just above the knee. Her hair was pulled back in a ponytail and her lips shone in a bright, enticing shade of red. Her brown eyes sparkled as she smiled and gestured for them to enter. "I'm so glad you're here, Tonya!" she exclaimed. "Everyone made it." Looking Ian up and down, she added, "Will your friend be participating?"

"Probably not, Liz," replied Tonya. "This is Ian. He thinks he likes me. I figured I'd prove him wrong. Would it be okay if he just watches?"

"Of course," she insisted. "But don't be too quick to write him off. He may surprise you."

"I'm pleased to meet you," offered Ian as he stepped in.

Liz shot him a tantalizing grin. "Do me a favor," she purred. "Surprise Tonya for me."

"Let's go, friend," chimed Tonya, grasping Ian's hand. "I'll show you around."

"I'll be there in a few minutes," answered Liz. "Jim's in the den."

Tonya showed Ian down a wide hallway to large, well-appointed room in the rear of the house, where more than two dozen people milled about, chatting with hors d'oeuvres and drinks to soft piano music. The crowd was exclusively couples. Much like Tonya, they struck Ian as everyday, ordinary folks, joking and laughing at a Saturday night get-together.

"C'mon," proposed Tonya, tugging his arm. I want you to meet Liz's husband. Stepping up to a fit, trim man in a business shirt and slacks, she asked, "Nervous, Jim?"

He drew in a deep breath. "I'd be lying if I said I wasn't," he admitted. "But I'm among friends, thanks to you. I can't believe you put this all together."

"It's gonna go fine," she assured him. "After this you'll see things in a new light. Say hi to Ian."

As Ian shook his hand, Tonya plopped onto a love seat and patted the sofa cushions on both sides. "Both of you sit," she insisted.

"Is this where the graduates from Mingling Singles go?" asked Ian as he sat to her left.

Tonya laughed aloud and pointed to the rear of the room, where a foot-high platform supported a king-size mattress appointed in heavy, deep blue sheets. The windows of the room were covered by thick, full-length drapes. Several large sofas and lounge chairs were arranged to face the makeshift nest.

"Care to guess again?" she asked.

"Karaoke?"

"Not even close."

"Wrestling?"

"Let's get ready to rumble," she purred as the lights dimmed.

Most of the guests found seats. The men who didn't stood behind their partners as Jim rose to his feet and cleared his throat. "Welcome everyone," he announced. "Liz and I are so glad you could all be here. We're truly honored to be a part of all this. We talked for a long time, but never thought such a thing could be properly organized...until we met Tonya, of course."

The guests applauded as Tonya stood and offered a shy wave. She sat back down and leaned against Ian, much to his happy surprise. As the room quieted, Jim stepped up to the platform and continued, "So, I apologize for not having much chance to get to know all of you. But I was talking to Tom and Lena, the hosts of next month's event. Liz and I are looking forward to being there and getting to know you all better after we've settled in. But for now, let's get started."

Liz appeared in the doorway, still in her black dress, but barefoot and without any jewelry. Her hair was down, draping over her thin shoulders as she stepped gracefully before the platform and faced Jim. After a quick kiss, she faced the guests as he stepped behind her.

"They're not gonna do it in front of everyone, are they?" asked Ian in a whisper.

Tonya giggled and snuggled in closer as Jim unzipped Liz's dress, lifted it over her head, and tossed it aside. The crowd offered polite applause as her perky breasts made their debut. They were medium size at best, but a perfect fit for her dainty torso. Her waist cambered to a delightful re-curve over her hips, and the bump of her tummy sat firm, adorned by the pea-size pit of her navel. She smiled and hooked her thumbs beneath her panties. The clapping continued as she tugged the dainty garment over her thighs and stepped out of it. Jim kissed Liz's neck and returned to the sofa, dropping the silky panties on Ian's lap as he passed. Liz stood before the guests naked, with her arms at her side.

Looking around the room, Ian realized about half the men were missing, but not for long. They filed in naked—a dozen in all. "Damn," he murmured under his breath, "I can't believe I'm just figuring this out."

"Leave now if it's too much," whispered Tonya. "Don't make a scene and ruin the night for everyone else."

Ian considered doing just that, but it wasn't him on display. It was a lovely brunette with long, lanky legs. Whatever her purpose, Tonya's touch was growing more magical by the moment. "I'll stick around," he said quietly.

"How bold of you," sassed Tonya, rubbing his thigh.

Like a kid in a movie theater on a first date, he snuck his arm around her. To his absolute elation, she leaned her head on his shoulder.

"Welcome," squeaked Liz in a nervous crackle as the men filed past her. "I'll do my best to remember names," she offered, turning her back to the crowd to face the men. "Danny, Jake, Jahleel, Sam and Marco, let's begin."

To Tonya's right, Jim peered on as the men stepped forward and formed a semi-circle around her. She knelt and sat back on her heels. Ian held his breath as she dunked over the rigid staff in the middle, stroking one on either side with each hand. He fought to keep his hand off his own crotch as he watched Liz's full black mane dance before the men's loins. He fought harder to keep it off Tonya's as Liz turned to her left and dunked over another beefy hard-on.

With Tonya nestled against his side, Ian watched Liz offer her wiles to one man after another, most often two at a time. She spent a good portion of the time on her elbows and knees, bobbing over one shaft while another thrust in and out of her from behind. Other times she rode atop her sex-mate, leaning forward to loll her tongue over a throbbing bulb or lick a cum-swollen sac.

On the other end of the sofa, Jim leaned forward and peered at a pearly ribbon dripping from his wife's slit. The scent of male pheromones filled the air as each new cock thrust into the remnants of its predecessor's seed. The sheets beneath her oozing crevice lay soaked with white puddles. Liz's lips glowed with mixed lineage as one chiseled shaft after another pulsed between them. Jim offered fist bumps as guys passed, returning to their wives after inseminating Liz and being replaced by a fresh stud from the floor.

Liz rolled onto her back and spread wide for a beefy, bronze-skinned hunk. As he sloshed into the concoction of proteins in her depths, Tonya brought her lips to Ian's ear. Her breath wafted like precious puffs of enchantment as she leaned the cleavage of her modest but firm breasts against his upper right arm. "Let's talk in the dining room," she whispered.

Ian followed her across the hallway and sat at the head of the handsome wooden table. Tonya took off her jacket and hung it on the back of a chair, then sat at the corner to his right. Her blue eyes sparkled as she gazed into his, folding her hands on the table. "Ian," she chimed, "the women at Mingling Singles are looking for love...someone to nest with and help raise their kids. They don't need guys looking to get their rocks off and move to the next. Let them be."

"So," he squeaked like a kid whose balls hadn't dropped. "You organize...these—"

"I organize all kinds of things, from ice cream socials to this and all things in between, like Mingling Singles. I thought you should see both ends of the spectrum. These are couples...mostly married ones. They're honest with themselves and each other about what excites them. I try to help them with that."

"Gangbangs excite them?"

"Raw sexual honesty excites them. It's not always a big gangbang. Jim and Liz have been kind of on the fringe for a while. They decided to do this to break the ice. This group gets together for social sexuality, and they wanted to be part of it. This is their offering to the assembly."

"Fair enough," he acknowledged, "But why did you bring me here?"

"Because you said you wanted to know me," snapped Tonya defensively. "If you really did, you'd have realized that these are my friends."

"Hold on!" he insisted. "You said you want someone to understand you. Maybe you should start by talking instead of accusing. What is it you want me to understand?"

"I'm sorry," she lamented, bowing her head. "I've never found a guy who was willing to even try to understand what's going on inside me." She took his hand and smiled. "Remember when I said you touched on something?" she asked.

"Did I touch on it again?"

Tonya nodded, then scooted over and sat on his lap. "People need all kinds of things," she explained. "Sometimes it's validation. Call me a slut or whatever, but I enjoy multiple partner sex. What I really want is someone to love me...to be my alpha. I want to watch other women enjoy him. I want them to know I'll share his sexuality, but that his love is mine. Is that so wrong?" She peered into his eyes as if looking for the answer in them. "Funny as it sounds," she added, "I'm loyal. I'll never kiss anyone but my lover."

"I think I get it. But it's a girl pulling that train, not a guy. What's Jim's deal? Is he a cuck?"

"Not at all. He finds it empowering, in fact. The women will offer themselves to him soon enough."

"Will you?"

"Hell yeah. He's hot." Bouncing to her feet, she offered her hand and urged, "Come watch again for a minute. I want you to see it like I do."

Ian followed her to the doorway. They paused, gazing in at Jim as he watched the umpteenth man of the evening plow his wife's pelvic garden. Liz lay on her back, legs spread for a rugged man with a broad chest. He held her ankles in his hands, arms outstretched as he reamed her. The sculptured vein lines of his cock glistened as he cycled, slapping his balls against her slit with each thrust.

"Look at Liz's face," proposed Tonya. "She's squinting. The corners of her mouth are dropped and her eyebrows are raised. She's embracing the instinct instilled in all living things at the

23

dawn of creation...the timeless need of the feminine to be seeded with new genealogy. Ancient societies honored the enchantment of amalgamation publicly as a celebration of life. Over time, the pompous and the pious have crafted social norms and relegated it to dark bedrooms and single partners, but we honor it."

Liz's sex-mate thrust forward and groaned. She sang out as he transferred the fruit of his balls into her intimate chamber. Moments later, she tipped her pelvis for her next partner.

"She's embracing it," admitted Ian. "But I'm still foggy on Jim's enthusiasm."

"Jim is Liz's alpha," chimed Tonya. "No one else kisses her. After everyone leaves, he'll enjoy planting his seed atop all the others." She snuggled up close and went on, "Look at her navel and imagine the billions of sperm teeming beneath it, swimming madly upstream as new rivals pour over them by the millions. Each one is striving to pass her cervix and enter her time machine to carry on its lineage. It wasn't a face that launched those thousand ships of lore. It was a womb...the grandest design of the Ultimate Architect." She grabbed his wrist and pulled his palm over her tummy. "How about you?" she asked. "Could you watch me be inseminated? Could you embrace it?"

"You-you get ganged on?"

"I have been, but it's not really my thing. Gangbangs are a bit busy and impersonal for me. I prefer smaller get-togethers, but I always find myself the fifth or seventh wheel."

"Tell me about the perfect get together," he requested.

A pleasant smile blessed her lips as she traced her finger on his chest. "My alpha and I are on a boat, or maybe at a mountain cabin. After we spend a day or two by ourselves, I invite...we invite a couple friend to join us. No pressure, no arranging, just wine and—"

Ian leaned in, but she turned her cheek. "I don't kiss on the first date," she whispered. "I told you how important it is to me."

"So you want an alpha who conforms to your rules?"

"Careful," she warned, lifting her chin. "I don't like to have my values challenged."

"Which is why you can't find the alpha you're looking for."

"So you're gonna get me to surrender to you?"

Bringing his nose an inch from hers, he replied, "You've been surrendering all night. You didn't want to tell me your name. Now you've admitted to liking gangbangs."

"I said I like intimate get-togethers."

Brushing his lips to hers, he replied, "I have a boat and a cabin."

"No you don't," she whispered into his mouth.

"Well, I have a canoe and a camper."

Her lips pressed against his with such perfect pressure he let out a whimper. "Is that your alpha warrior call?" she asked in a purr before resuming their kiss.

He hummed in his deepest tone as his tongue met hers in ideal cadence. "That's better," she whispered, blessing his jaw with caressing fingers. A needy peep escaped her as his hands caressed her backside. "I'm done here if you'd like to come by my place," she tendered.

"Aren't you needed here?" he asked.

"I organized it well. They'll be fine. Besides, think of what the cleanup entails."

Ian looked into the crowd to see hair dancing over men's laps and women, still clad in skirts and dresses, bounding atop their mates. Not knowing the group, he had no way of determining whether the copulating couples had arrived together. "Right behind you," he acknowledged.

"So just to clarify," he asked as they snuck out the front door. "This will be one on one?"

"I'd better make sure you're up to my friends' standards," she sassed.

****

Half an hour later, Ian followed Tonya to the front door of her modest split-level home. She pulled his arm, leading him through the kitchen and down the hall to the bedroom. "So help me," she warned, closing the door. "You'd better not be the guy I thought you were earlier."

"What's that supposed to mean?"

"It means I saw you looking at the refrigerator."

"Maybe I was hungry."

"Or maybe you were looking for kid's schoolwork stuck on magnets."

"Can you blame me?"

"I guess not. Now take off your clothes."

"You first, miss no kissing on the first date."

"Fine," she quipped, tossing her sleeveless white blouse on the floor.

Ian froze at the sight of her naked torso. It was no different than a plethora of others he had seen in his lifetime. Her waist cambered sweetly beneath her ribcage like any girl with a thin, petite build. The pit of her navel sat on the bump of her belly between lean but capable hips, like a thousand girls at the beach on a sunny day. But it was her torso—Tonya Forsythe's being. It was the vessel that encapsulated her actuality and housed her vital, life-giving parts. In the few short hours since they met, that being had become precious. He stood statue-still, his lower lip trembling.

Tonya gave a knowing smile. "I guess you do see something in me," she offered, dropping her yoga pants and panties.

Unbuttoning his shirt and tossing it aside, Ian gaped at her well-trimmed, strawberry blonde bush. Tonya unbuttoned his pants as he kicked his shoes off. Her eyes studied his rock-hard staff as he sat on the edge of the bed. Dropping to her knees, she brought her lips to his aching bulb, wrapping her palm around his chiseled girth. "What does my alpha want?" she asked as his prowess thumped in her palm.

"Someone who doesn't need to ask what I want," he replied in a gasping grunt.

She touched her nose to his engorged knob then pressed it against his belly, shifting her gaze up to his eyes. Peering through his pupils and into his thoughts, she lashed his upper length with licks as his moans grew higher in pitch. Cupping his tingling jewels in her palm, she lunged over half his length.

Ian let out an elated groan as the moist warmth of her mouth registered in his conscience. His balls went to work between her playful fingers as the vacuum of her cheeks drew pangs of wanton delight through his length. Tonya hummed softly as her lips travelled over the sculpted vein lines of his cock. Her cheek quivered as she stopped to loll her tongue on his knob.

When she came up for air, he jumped to his feet and lifted her up, setting her on the edge of the bed and kneeling between her thighs. She squealed as he wrapped his forearms under the backs of her thighs and pressed his nose into the scruff of her bikini-trimmed bush. Her scent was one of sheer delight—rich with estrogen and feminine fervency. She cooed as his tongue parted her labial gates and dashed into the nectar of her welcoming crevice.

The glorious taste of her inner tissues lived up to their delightful aroma. Wiggling his tongue into her, he swept the length of her entrance to peeps of delight. With careful calculation, he worked his way up to the pronounced bud of her erect clitoris.

"Huh!" she wailed. "I have to warn you, I'm a squirter!"

Ian hummed into her pelvis and dug into her again.

Tonya's thighs trembled as he tipped her undulating pelvis. She bucked back and forth, seemingly uncontrolled as a long, low moan emanated from her chest. It grew to a high pitch squeak as a gush of reward sprayed his neck and pectorals. A second wash greeted him as he lunged over her blushing apex. She wiggled like a worm on a hook as Ian lapped up what he could of his efforts.

"Usually only girls can do that to me," she grunted. "Get inside me!"

For no other reason than to show off, he stood and scooped her up, holding her by the sides of the torso. She threw her arms over his shoulders and wrapped her legs around his back as he shifted his hands down to her firm, fit buttocks. Peering into her deep blue eyes, he lowered her onto the tip of his throbbing cock, bathing the skin of his bulb in the slick heat of her clench.

Tonya cooed as her clasp widened in accommodation. With the rim of his crown ensconced in the velvet grasp of her love channel, he let gravity impale her on his pole. They sang together as their pubic hairs meshed. Buried in the hug of her heavenly hollow, he pressed his lips to hers and offered his tongue.

Breaking their kiss, Ian lifted her high and stood her beside the bed. With a playful purr, she turned her back to him and leaned forward, rolling her hips. As Ian grasped her waist, she stood on her toes. Already coated in her love juices, his rigid shaft met no resistance as he sheathed it in her precious frame and broke into rhythm.

"Yes, yes, oh yes!" sang Tonya as his pelvis slapped off her buttocks. She straightened her back, offering unhindered access to her depths as he cycled in and out of her divine chamber. Two dozen or so strokes later, she lunged forward and curved her back like a feline, spraying his thighs in a squeal of wanton release. She scampered onto the bed as another gush soaked the sheets. Rolling onto her back, she circled her finger around her gush button and flailed her legs as if she was being hung. "Come in me!" she pleaded. "I want your sperm swimming inside me!"

Ian climbed between her legs, planted his plow, and grasped her calves. Tonya cried out as he rocked his hips, again burying his entirety in her welcoming heat. She dug her heels into the mattress and arched, raising her loins off the sheets. Pangs of nirvana twanged through Ian's buried beam as he drove into the enchantment of her inners. He let out a surrendering grunt, falling forward onto his hands.

Tonya dropped her buttocks and wrapped him tight with her legs. "Come in me!" she squealed, "Shoot your cum deep inside me!"

Ian dropped to his elbows and kissed her as the tingling voltage of bliss thumped through his shaft, pumping his pedigree into the vault of her intimacy in a succession of viscous jets. She squealed to the beat as each seedy salvo sprayed into the garden of her actuality.

But Ian's heaving head refused to cease its inseminating eruption. Perhaps in a bid to outdo any future rival, or group of them, his thumping cock continued its deluge, swathing her inners in jets of potency. Tonya spread wide and broke their kiss, screaming the name of the creator as the irrigation of her challis continued. Finally—almost thankfully, the sperm-laden assault faded to spurts, then bumps. With his blissful transfer complete, Ian gave her a quick kiss and rolled onto his side.

"Good lordie-lou!" she exclaimed. "Should I expect that every time?"

"You wanted alpha," he blurted, heaving for air.

"Who needs gangbangs with a fire hose like that spraying their walls? I might keep you all to myself."

"That's it," he joked. "I'm going back to Mingling Singles."

"Uh," she moaned spreading her legs and pushing out a gob of goo. As it oozed into the cleft of her buttocks, she purred, "You're right. I gotta show you off." Bringing her lips to his, she whispered, "I wish one of my girlfriends was here to dig her tongue into me right now."

"That's something I'd love to see."

"Better yet, I'd like to watch you brew another batch and top her off so I could eat it out of her."

Ian's flaccid mast grew back to rock-hard readiness as she kissed him. Reaching down, she stroked him gently. "Save it, big fella," she purred. "It's two in the morning. Stay here tonight and I'll have a couple over tomorrow evening. I've got a friend who's been dying for me to meet her boyfriend."

"I'll make supper," he offered. "Maybe salmon on the grill?"

"An alpha who cooks," she replied with a giggle. "Looks like I hit the jackpot. Deanne will be impressed."

"Deanne?"

"You'll like her. She's feisty. I hear her boyfriend Cliff's a hot ticket, too."

"I'll bet he is," replied Ian as she snuggled up to his shoulder and closed her eyes.

The Right Conversation (Threesomes)

A young couple talks openly about threesomes.

"Have you ever had a threesome?" Devon asked his girlfriend of six months, Traci. This question was not random or from out of the blue. Devon and Traci had agreed to be open and honest with each other about sex. Topics included their pasts, their desires, likes and dislikes and their fantasies. They decided to talk about anything and not to judge each other. They would have no secrets and hide nothing from each other. If either of them asked a question, they would answer it.

It started a few weeks ago. Things had been getting pretty serious between the two of them, and they were committed to making their relationship the best it could be. They felt that total honesty was critical. It started out fairly innocently, with a question here, a story there, but it quickly developed into something fun and exciting for them both. They referred to it as "the conversation."

Traci grinned at her boyfriend as she thought back to her past. "Sort of, but not exactly," she answered, ambiguously.

"What does that mean?" Devon asked, playfully laughing as he put his arms around his girlfriend and pulled her closer to him on their bed. They'd just finished having sex, which usually was when they had the conversation.

Traci adjusted the pillows behind her head, then leaned closer to Devon, putting her head on his chest. She ran her fingers lightly over his chest and teased his nipple.

"Well," she began, "it was just one time, during the summer after graduating from high school. You remember I told you about my boyfriend back then, Tony?"

"Yeah," Devon replied, stroking her arm lovingly. "The jock, right?"

"Yep, that's him," she said, continuing her story, "We were over at my friend Kim's house. She had a big pool in her backyard that overlooked a lake. It was on a big wooded lot and very private."

"Sounds great, but what happened?" Devon asked impatiently.

"I'm getting there," she replied, then pinched his nipple hard.

"Oww!" he blurted out, chuckling.

"So, it was hot, and we were young. We had been drinking some beers, and I'm pretty sure we had smoked some pot. Kim's dad was a major pothead, and she always had the best weed. We were all feeling pretty relaxed and mellow, so we decided to go skinny dipping."

"Kim was adorable. She was short but had big tits and ass. Tony was impressed, and his dick got hard. He had a very athletic body with lots of muscles, but his dick was kind of average, much smaller than this."

She reached down and squeezed Devon's plump, recently fucked cock, then waved it back and forth. It swung in her hands as she shook it, the head flopping left and right.

"Sucks to be him," Devon chuckled. "Go on, please."

"Well, one thing led to another. Tony and I were getting frisky on a lounger. Kim was sitting and watching as I sucked his dick. He was fingering me. I noticed he was watching Kim, so I checked out what she was doing. She was lying there facing us, with her legs wide open, fingering her pussy."

"Did that turn you on or piss you off?" Devon asked. His cock was stirring to life due to the combination of her hand action and her story.

"I thought it was hot," she said, grinning. "Tony thought so too. I got a wild idea and invited Kim to come over and suck his dick.

39

She jumped at the chance. I held it for her as she started, but soon she was deep throating it, and I let go."

Traci slid her face down and wrapped her lips around the head of Devon's cock. She jacked it several times, as it grew fully erect, then licked around the head making Devon groan softly. She pulled her mouth off, giggling, and caressed his dick as she continued talking.

"She was better at sucking it than I was," she said as her fist pumped up and down.

"You're very good at it now," Devon said through clenched teeth.

"I've had more practice since then," she said with a wink. "So, I watched how she sucked Tony and how much he liked it. I let her keep doing it. She was on her hands and knees on the lounger, between his legs, sitting on her feet. I sat next to them, kissing Tony as he had one hand on my breast and the other on one of Kim's, massaging them both."

"I scooted as close to them as I could and rubbed my pussy. I turned my head, laying it on Tony's chest, watching her mouth go up and down his shaft. I was fucking turned on. Tony was groaning, and he removed his hand from Kim's tit to put it on the back of her head, pushing her down more. She moaned and started sucking him even more aggressively."

Traci took Devon's prick back into her mouth and sucked it hungrily, pushing her mouth all the way down to the base, deep throating him easily. She lifted up, letting his cock slide slowly out of her mouth, coated with her saliva.

"I thought Kim looked incredibly hot sucking my boyfriend's dick. I pulled my hand off my pussy and rubbed my wet fingers on Kim's nipple. She whimpered and started shaking. I'd never touched her or any other girl like that. Her reaction turned me on even more. I sat up next to her, sliding my hand down her back and over her ass. As I did, she reached between my legs and pushed a finger inside me. I got up on my knees beside her and spread my legs to give her more access.

"I slid my fingers down the crack of her ass. It felt warm and smooth. My finger brushed over her puckery asshole, and she squealed. I moved my hand lower, finding her pussy. Thick, mucus-like fluid was dripping from her. I pushed two fingers inside. She moaned around Tony's cock and lifted her hips up so that she was on her hands and knees."

"I used my fingers to fuck her pussy. I didn't know what I was doing, but I was on fire with lust. I fingered her the way I like to have my pussy fingered when I'm that horny. I jammed my fingers in and out of her pussy rapidly. Her juices were flowing through my fingers and dripping from my hand. I pulled my fingers out and rubbed them against her clit, letting it slip between my index and middle fingers, pinching it between them as my fingers moved back and forth."

"Tony groaned loudly and cried out that he was going to cum. He was warning her to stop before he came in her mouth, but Kim only whimpered again and sucked him harder. He yelled loudly and came, shooting his cum in my best friend's mouth. Kim swallowed as fast as she could, but a lot of his sperm ran down her chin and his cock. Before he finished cumming, Kim started squealing and bouncing her pussy up and down against my hand. She came and came and came."

Traci resumed sucking Devon's cock, using her tongue along the underside to add extra stimulation as her mouth worked it up and down. He put his hand on her head, pushing it down like Tony had done Kim. He thrust up into her mouth, fucking her face as she deepthroated him.

"Ugh," Devon groaned, "I'm cumming! Fuck!"

Traci lifted her body up, pushing her mouth down entirely. Devon's cock head pushed into her throat as the first blast of semen shot out. She swallowed. He cried out more, hand gripping her hair in his fist.

"Ohh, fuck Traci," he shouted, "suck it! Suck it! Suck! It!"

He fired more and more cum into her throat and mouth. She kept her mouth around his dick until he stopped shooting sperm. She slowly pulled off, swirled the remaining cum around in her mouth savoring his taste, then swallowed it.

"Wow, that was a lot of cum, Devon," she said, wiping her chin and licking the remnants off her fingers. "I guess you liked my story."

He chuckled hard. "Oh fuck yes," he said, trying to catch his breath, "that was hot. So, then what happened?"

She grinned up at him, still holding his dick, which hung limply in her little fist. She licked a little bit of cum off the tip. "Kim's dad came home then, and we all had to scamper wildly to get dressed and hide the empty beer cans."

"So you didn't get to cum?" Devon asked stroking her cheek lovingly.

"No, those greedy bastards got off and left poor little me to masturbate once I got home."

"So, is that the only time you had a threesome?" he asked as he pulled her up to lay next to her.

She cuddled against him, idly stroking the small amount of hair in the center of his chest. "Just that one time. How about you? You ever have a threesome?"

"Me?" Devon asked as if there was someone else in the room that she could have been asking. "No, I was never that lucky. I dated a girl that offered it once with her cousin, but we broke up before we ever did it."

"Awww, poor baby," she said, lifting up to kiss him. "Is it on your bucket list?"

He smiled after kissing her, tasting a faint trace of the mustiness of his cum, but ignoring it. "Yeah, it is. Hopefully one day I'll get the opportunity. What about with two men? You ever do that?"

She rolled slightly more onto her belly, her chin laying on his chest and looked up into his eyes. "No, only in my fantasies," she said with a naughty grin.

"Oh?" he asked, raising his eyebrows, "Is that on your bucket list?"

Her grin grew into a full smile, and she felt herself blushing. "Maybe," she whispered.

Devon gave her a playful scowl. "Ahem," he chided her playfully, "Full honesty, remember?"

Traci bit her bottom lip and nodded. "Ok, in the spirit of honesty, let me tell you. First, the idea of having sex with two men at the same time is one of my favorite fantasies. It is right up there with Dirty Santa. I masturbate to it frequently, and that kind of porn can get me going more than anything."

"Dirty Santa?" Devon asked, pretending to be shocked. "What's that?"

"It's just a silly fantasy a lot of girls get. You know, Dirty Santa sneaks into the house at night. Dirty Santa finds you touching yourself and asks if you're naughty or nice. Dirty Santa says he has something better than a lump of coal for girls on the naughty list. Dirty Santa pulls his cock out and has you sit on his lap as you tell him what you want for Christmas. Dirty Santa cums in your pussy, then leaves you with a new Barbie Doll, eats the cookie you made for him, drinks the milk and goes back up the chimney, leaving you with a little elf growing inside you. Typical, everyday fantasy."

Devon stared at her. "Uhm, ok. I could have gone the rest of my life without knowing about that. Now, I'm never going to look at Santa the same."

"Oh, no, you'll look at him the same way I do," she giggled, "I love to go to the store in a skirt with no panties and sit on Santa's lap."

"Do you really?" Devon asked, this time in real shock.

Traci giggled and waggled her eyebrows up and down. "If I'm still letting you date me at Christmas time, you can find out for yourself."

"Letting me?" he asked, pulling her closer for a kiss, "Don't you mean if I let you?"

She kissed him then pulled back, "No, I know you want me too much. You're hooked. I'm still on the fence about you."

He gave her a dirty look. "Really? What would you need to decide to keep me? As long as we both shall live?"

Her breath caught in her throat. "Did you just ask me to marry you?"

"Maybe," he said, blushing.

"Ahem," she chided, "what happened to full honest?

"Oh yeah, I forgot," Devon said, kissing her forehead. "I guess then, yeah, I did just ask you to marry me."

She turned her head and laid it back on his chest, kissing his nipple softly. "Cool," she whispered, "I like that."

"That's all you can say?" he asked, teasing her.

"Well, yeah. If you actually want me to answer that question, you're going to have to do a better job of asking it, with the proper equipment."

Devon stroked her hair tenderly. "Well, assuming I had the right equipment and asked you properly, what would your answer be?"

"Hypothetically?" she asked her fingertip writing words on his chest.

"Hypothetically," he answered.

"Full honesty?" she asked as she finished writing the word 'yes.'

"Full honesty," he said.

"I just wrote the answer on your chest," she said, kissing his chest. "You'll have to read it to figure it out. If you can't read it, then I guess you'll have to ask me properly."

"With the proper equipment?" he asked.

"Of course!" she said looking him in the eyes, then kissing his nose. "Didn't you want to hear the rest of my answer about if having two men is on my bucket list?"

He grinned, knowing she was changing the subject. She'd practically confirmed that she would accept if he proposed. He was delighted, and the post-orgasmic bliss had flooded his brain with endorphins. "Yes, I'm sorry to have distracted you. Please continue."

"I love you, Devon," she said, "but having sex with anyone other than you is not on my bucket list. It is not something I would ever do or have any interest in pursuing."

"Oh," he said, sounding somewhat disappointed. "Why is that? You said it's your most popular fantasy next to Dirty Santa."

"It's close, but nothing beats my Santa," she giggled, "But, the thing about threesomes or sex with other people, which I learned the hard way, is that something that is great as a fantasy, never ends well in reality."

"What do you mean?" he asked, "Did something happen after the threesome that makes you think that?"

"Yes, something did happen. So, a couple of weeks after the threesome, I was supposed to be working, but the power was out at Starbucks, and they sent us home. I called Tony to get together because I knew he had the day off. With college coming, we only had a few more days before we had to go to other towns. He had tried to get me not to go in so that we could spend the day fucking, but I needed the money. Since I was free, I wanted to meet and ride his cock one last time before we had to move."

"When he didn't answer my calls and texts, I was bummed out. I was bored so, I called up Kim. Oddly, she didn't answer either. I knew she was home, so I drove over to her house. I was surprised when I saw Tony's car in the driveway. I parked

49

behind him and walked around to the back of the house. I saw a couple of empty beer cans on the deck next to the pool and his swimming trunks lying near a discarded bikini."

"I had a bad feeling in the pit of my stomach. I walked up to the stairs to the upper-level deck that opened into the family room and the bedrooms along the back of their house. The family room was all windows and sliding doors that gave a great view of the lake. As I reached the top of the stairs, I saw them. Kim was laying on the couch, her back against the armrest. She was naked and had her legs spread wide, knees bent, feet wrapped around Tony's ass as he fucked her hard."

"I stood there, frozen, staring, unable to look away for a couple of minutes. The funny thing was, I didn't care that Tony was fucking her. What hurt was the lying and the betrayal, the cheating and excluding me from the activity."

"After a few minutes, I took out my phone and snapped a couple of pictures of them, then turned and walked away. I got in my car and texted them both a message with the pictures attached. The message to Kim said, 'you can have him.' The message to Tony said 'have a nice life'"

"It was an hour before either of them tried to call or text me. The first to reach me was Kim she was crying and apologetic, but I told her she was no longer my friend. Friends don't fuck their boyfriends behind their back. She tried to rationalize her behavior, but I just hung up on her. I never spoke to her again."

"Tony called, but I never answered. He showed up at my house trying to talk to me. I just told him it was over. We were leaving for different colleges in a couple of days. There was no point in trying to keep things going anyway. But, since he had proved to be a worthless shit, we should end it right away. He got pissed, grabbed onto me and tried to drag me into his car. If my father hadn't come running out, I don't know what might have happened. In any event, it ended badly."

"Wow," Devon said, stroking her with love, "I'm sorry you had to have something like that happen. But, that wasn't really a threesome, they were cheating. I mean, if they had joined with you, it would have been ok, right?"

Traci shook her head. "No, I think you misunderstood me. It wasn't that them fucking without me was why I was upset. We could have done that, I suppose. However, it wouldn't have changed anything. My point is we had a threesome. When we did, we crossed a line that could not be uncrossed. Once you go there, you can't go back. What we did together was not cheating, but it opened the door for them. It made them feel that it was okay for them to fuck without, because why not? They'd already

51

messed around with me. Surely I wouldn't care if they did, right?"

"I mean, our having that threesome tore down a wall of propriety that had existed as a boundary. Without it, there were no more boundaries. Infidelity came easier, almost naturally."

"I think I see what you mean," Devon said, "but that doesn't necessarily have to happen if the couple believes in open communication and full honesty, like us, right?"

"It becomes hard to stay honest when your feelings lead you away from that kind of pure relationship," she replied.

"I don't understand," Devon said, fingers lightly scratching her scalp and massaging her head.

"When you start to feel things for another person, you find yourself caught in a dilemma. You want what you want, but you don't want to lose what you have. You start to realize that a white lie here, leaving out a few details there, allows you to have your cake and eat it too."

"But, not if it's just sex," Devon countered. "Right?"

"When is sex ever just sex?" Traci replied. "If you want sex without feeling something, then masturbate. Hire a hooker. We want sex because we want to have incredible sex, not just biological relief. We want mind-shattering, earth-blowing, gut-wrenching powerful sex. If not, why bother?"

"Yeah, I suppose so," he conceded. "But, how is that a problem?"

"There are so many different ways that is a problem, Devon. First of all, I want that kind of sex to be with you. I want to share that feeling, to cum that hard, to be totally into the sexual surrender so that my entire being is overpowered with the bliss and joy of orgasm, with you. To me, sexual arousal and orgasm is the same feeling, the same energy as love. It is the ultimate manifestation of love."

"I agree," he said, considering her words. "I still don't see the problem."

"Would you care if another man fucked me?" Traci asked point blank.

"That depends," he said.

"On what?"

"Well, I think it depends on your motivation for doing it, if I was I included, would I know in advance and approve of it, that kind of thing." Devon was struggling to answer adequately, but trying hard to make his point.

"Ok, so remember a couple of days ago, you called and said you would be late getting home? You got home around 7:30, but I wasn't here when you got back. I came home about 9:00, a little tipsy."

"I'd say more like hammered than tipsy, but yeah, I remember. What about it?" Devon asked looking at Traci suspiciously.

"I told you that I went to dinner with Jenny from work, that we'd had a few glasses of wine and lost track of time, right?"

"Yeah, that's right."

"You believed me. What would you feel if I told you that it was a lie? What if instead, I'd been out with Mike from work, got drunk at his apartment and had sex with him? How would you feel?"

"Wait," he said nervously, "are you trying to tell me you cheated on me?" He quickly got angry, "What the fuck, Traci?"

She raised her head and shushed him. "No, silly," she said softly, "of course, not. But, see. You would be angry and hurt, right?"

"Yes, of course!" he shouted, "And I'd beat his fucking ass if he touched you."

"But, what if I invited Mike over here and fucked him in front of you? What if I told you that it was my hottest fantasy ever, to make you watch as Mike pounds my pussy?"

"I'd be pissed! That's not a threesome either!"

"But, really it's the same thing, right. If I fucked Mike without you there, in front of you or with your blessing, I'd still be fucking Mike. He'd still be making me cum. He'd still be putting his seed inside me. He'd still be doing things to me that you aren't."

Devon slowly nodded, "Yeah, ok. I see that. I still think it's different, but I see the similarities."

Traci changed her direction a little, still trying to get Mike to understand.

"Who is the best lover you've ever had?" she asked him smiling expectantly.

"You are," he replied, grinning, "without a doubt."

"Ok, either you're a sweetheart or a good liar," she said winking, "but since we believe in full honesty, I believe you." She kissed him softly on the lips. "And by the way, you're the best lover I've ever had."

"That's good to know," he said.

"But, you know, I've been thinking. I've not fucked that many people in my life. You're like the fifth guy I've ever had sex with. Out of the billions of people on the planet, five is a pretty small number."

"Yeah, that's true," he said, staring at her and wondering where she was going.

"So, maybe you're only the best lover of the five I've had. Who's to say that mystery man number eight might not be better than you? Maybe, in reality, you suck at fucking, but you're better than the shitty lovers I've had before. Now that I think about it, I watched some of these cuckolding videos where some stranger, usually black fuck the wife. They get fucked so hard, so wildly and they cum uncontrollably. They completely lose control of their minds because the sex is that good. You've never fucked me like that. You've never made me cum like that. Maybe I need one of them. Maybe I should get some big black cock to pound this pussy in ways you can't even imagine. I mean you want me to be happy and have the best sex I can, right? So, maybe I should stop fucking you and go out and fuck as many guys as I can, hoping to find a guy who is better than you."

"Jesus Christ, Traci," Devon declared, pushing her off him and sitting up to stare at her angrily. "What the fuck is getting into you? Is that how you feel?"

Traci smiled and shook her head, "No, baby, not at all. I'm just trying to make a point. Sex with you is the best I've ever had. I love it. I want it just to get better and better. It is. Every time we have sex it is better than the last time. Yeah, I may not cum like those porno sluts, but half of that shit is fake. But, I believe that there's nothing to stop us both from being able to have that kind of strong orgasms, especially if we are open about our feelings."

"Damn, girl," he said, "don't scare me like that. Yeah, I agree. It does get better, and I want to find ways to make you cum like that. That's why I thought if we have a threesome, you will get to experience that kind of feeling."

"But, then it wouldn't be YOU making me feel it, Devon," she explained. "It would be some other guy."

"Right, I get that, I think," he said, "I mean, I'd be a part of it, though."

"Yeah but there are a few things that I see as huge risks: 1) what if the guy makes me cum like that... fucks me that well, do you think I could experience that from someone and NOT start to have immediate feelings for him?"

"Uhh, I don't know. I hadn't thought about it."

"And if we do it more than once, the feelings would get stronger and stronger and stronger until one day, he's not fucking me anymore, he's making love to me. Then what?"

"Yeah, that would suck," he admitted.

"2) how could I get fucked like that and experience that kind of pleasure and not want it more and more and more. From him or from guys even bigger and better than him. What if you don't want me to? Would I feel the need so strongly that I'd do it behind your back?"

"Yeah, I can see that happening," he said, "You're right."

"And 3) if you saw me, the woman you love, your best lover, being fucked like that, being pleasured like that, wouldn't your feelings for me change? Wouldn't you feel at some level I had betrayed you or that you had lost me? Would you feel inadequate the next time you try to fuck me? Wouldn't you worry that you're not good enough for me or that I wish he was fucking me and not you?"

"Wow," he said, breathing hard, "yeah, I see that. Damn, Traci. I hadn't thought of any of this stuff. I just thought it was sex. Just sex. We'd still be us. We'd be unchanged."

"You can't do something like that and not change. It's the boundaries. They're gone. Once you cross that line, everything else becomes easy to do. Cheating. Lying. Deception. Infidelity."
"Yeah, fuck," he said hugging Traci tightly, "you're right. Man, I can't believe I didn't see that."

"So, do you want to know what happened with Kim and Tony?" Traci asked after giving Devon a gentle kiss.

"I'm not sure I do," he said chuckling.

"Well, I'm going to tell you," she said giving him a dirty look, "Kim transferred to his college after one semester. They moved in together. After graduation, they got married."

"Wow," he said, "all because you had a threesome by the pool?"

"That was the catalyst, yes," Traci replied, "but that's not the end of the story. Kim got pregnant, and they had a baby girl. Except, the baby was not Tony's. Tony and Kim were both white, and her baby was as black as black can be. It turns out that Kim had developed a taste for black cocks after they had a threesome with a black guy for 'just sex.'"

"No shit?" he said.

"So, yeah," Traci concluded, "Having a threesome with two guys is a hot as hell fantasy. We can roleplay it. You can buy a big black dildo and fuck me with it as you pretend its another guy. But, I will never have sex with anyone but you, ever. Don't suggest it. Don't beg for it. It will not happen." She kissed him again, then smiled lovingly paraphrasing the wedding vows from their favorite TV show, Game of Thrones.

"I am yours, and you are mine, from this day until the end of my days, so get used to that idea, mister."

Devon kissed her and nodded happily. "So, does that mean yes?"

"Full honesty?" she asked, smiling brightly.

"Full honesty," Devon replied tenderly brushing the hair from her face.

"In full honesty, the answer is yes," Traci replied, raising up to kiss him.

Farting During Anal Sex (Anal Sex)

A woman's guide to anal sex etiquette.

Folks, I have something to confess. I simply cannot keep it locked inside me anymore. It's tearing me apart, eating me alive from the inside out and I must uburden my soul. And I am not the sort of man easily given to confessionals. I have been called a sociopath in the past because I feel that guilt is the weakest sensation a man can ever feel. I'm not a sociopath. I care about certain things, like myself, for example. I also like music, and literature. I don't much care for other humans unless I want sex or money from them. Does that make me remorseless? I think not. However, I feel that the time has come for me to come clean about my most forbidden special interests and illicit activities. Here goes nothing, folks. This confession of mine is not for the faint-hearted or softy type of people out there. No sir. It's for hardcore people. Anyhow, you asked for it. You got it. This is the story of my dark confessions.

I like fucking big women in the ass. It doesn't matter what their race, religion, profession, political affiliation or marital status is. My only requirement, or preference is more like it, is that they are large and curvy. Why big women? I don't know. I've always felt attracted to big women. I've never looked at a skinny woman in my life, except maybe to identify one in a police lineup. My attraction to big women is emotional and physical, but mainly sexual in nature. I'll tell you a little secret. Big girls have extremely tight assholes. It's something most people simply do not know. Well, I do. And I love anal sex with large women. Just bend them over, spread their butt cheeks and shove my cock deep down where the sun doesn't shine. Is that a crime? I think not!

My name is Dale Alton. Black college man extraordinaire, con artist and vagabond. Six feet two inches tall, lean and muscular, with dark brown skin, a clean-shaven, handsome face and golden brown eyes. I have long hair braided into dreadlocks. A part-time student at Devon College in Ohio, USA. I major in Criminal Pathology. Oh, and I am also a sportsman. Devon College sponsors Men's Baseball, Soccer, Basketball, Rugby, Bowling, Tennis, Golf, Cross Country, Ice Hockey, Wrestling, Swimming and Football along with Women's Basketball, Bowling, Soccer, Field Hockey, Lacrosse, Softball, Ice Hockey, Tennis, Golf, Rugby and Swimming. I am a running back on the Football team. It's alright, I guess. This isn't a sports story by any chance. Not unless deep and raunchy anal sex became an intercollegiate sport, in which case I would be the undisputed champion of all divisions. Without challenge. Why? I am the King of Anal Sex! The undisputed master of fucking women in the ass. With or without lube. End of story!

Currently, I'm hanging out with my fuck buddy Amy Stoltz. She's a big and plump white chick with long blonde hair and pale green eyes. This big-bottomed female is an anal sex enthusiast, which is what I love about her. Presently speaking, she's on all fours, her plump butt cheeks spread wide open. Sliding in and out of her tight asshole is my twelve-inch, uncut black super cock. This looked like a fine end to a fine day. Amy was shy about sex at first but I quickly turned her into a sex-craving nymphomaniac and an anal slut. I simply brought out the side of her which she repressed the most. I let her freak flag fly. And I got to fuck her in the ass. Repeatedly.

As we fucked, I found myself having quite a lot of fun. Amy was a thick woman with a big butt yet her asshole was wonderfully warm and tight. I placed my hands on Amy's wide hips and pushed my cock deeper into her asshole. Oh, man. I can barely describe to you how it feels. Shoving your cock into a woman's asshole is one of life's greatest pleasures. Something that should be treasured when it happens for the first time and savored again and again. I'm the world's most dedicated ass fucker. Plowing my cock deep into the butt holes of women of all races sinc e my nineteenth year upon this earth. It's not something which I see myself tiring of any time soon.

Anal sex is addictive. Especially when you're doing it with the likes of Amy, America's favorite voluptuous anal slut. Amy is fond of saying that she can handle any cock size in that wonderfully tight yet marvelously expandable asshole of hers. Well, today was the day that I put it to the test. You know what that means. I'm going to ram my twelve inches of hard black cock into her tight asshole. Deep into the forbidden depths of her booty hole which I am going to stretch to the limit. I am going to see what the inside of her asshole looks like. Sans lube. Think she can handle an anal sex challenge of that magnitude? It's just about time to find out. Let the anal fun and games begin.

I took Amy's hands and held them behind her back. Then I pushed her down on the dorm room floor. Face down and big ass up. That's how I liked her to be. I only wished she could be like that every moment of every day. Unfortunately, it's not going to happen anytime soon. I spread Amy's plump butt cheeks to a width that I'm pretty sure they've never reached before. I looked at that tight pink asshole of hers. Nice. I spat and rubbed it all over the tiny asshole. Then, I pressed my cock against her asshole. With a swift thrust, I went in. I pushed my cock deep into her asshole. What a purely satisfying sensation. I only wished I could share it with you. The asshole of a woman is much tighter than her pussy will ever be. So, it's always more satisfying for a man to stick his cock up a woman's asshole than into her pussy. A simple fact which you won't read anywhere.

With that, I pushed my cock deeper into Amy's butt hole. Into depths which had never before been explored. She squealed as I rammed my cock into her asshole. Laughing, I grabbed a handful of her long blonde hair and yanked her head back while drilling my cock into the most forbidden depths of her tight asshole. I fucked her ass mercilessly. Until she begged for mercy. I fucked her so good that she lost it and fucking farted. Could you believe it? Amy farted during anal sex! The big girl farted with my cock still in her ass. I laughed as she turne d red from embarassment. I decided to give her a lesson in anal sex etiquette. I made her say some rather memorable phrases while getting fucked in the ass. I Shall Not Fart During Anal Sex Ever Again. We continued romping away happily until I finally came, sending my hot cum deep inside her asshole. Amy howled. I roared victoriously. It was music to my ears. Slowly, I pulled out of her. What I saw amazed me. Amy's booty hole was now a gaping hole. Stretched wide open by my mercilessly anal fucking. I smiled as I admired my handiwork. I felt so proud. I smacked her ass and she yelped. I grinned. This was a good day.

A short while later, Amy and I parted ways. I felt the plump white chick happy as a clown in her dorm. I would be back for more raunchy and sheer nasty fun later. All was right with the world. I went back to my dorm to watch my favorite Friday night television shows on USA Network and Sci-Fi. I love action comedies like Monk and Psych along with science fiction thrillers like Stargate Atlantis, Flash Gordon and Kindred : The Embraced. Can't get enough of them. Anyhow, got places to go an

A Sneak Attack (Taboo Sex)

He takes an opportunity to pleasure his taboo lover.

We've had this secret for a while now. We're not supposed to share our bodies the way we do. We know it's wrong. But we love it. And we love that it's wrong. That's probably why it's so intense every single time our skin makes contact.

For the past two weeks, we've been stuck in this house, unable to do anything but sneak a few quick kisses behind a door or a quick flash of your breasts from a shadowy corner.

This isn't supposed to be happening. You and I aren't supposed to be passionate lovers. But we are. We sneak looks across the room. Our fingers secretly graze across each other's exposed skin in passing, or under the table.

I'm not sure I can take it any longer. Being this close to you for so long has me in a constant state of arousal. My cock is heavy over sensitive. Every time I move I'm completely aware of how it's resting against me and trapped inside my pants. My balls are swollen with unspent loads intended for you, my forbidden lover. I can feel the constant bubbling of precum slipping from the head. It soaked into my boxer briefs and moistens the inner portion of my thigh. The thought of it being noticed should terrify me. But in truth it only makes me hornier as I day dream of continuing our torrid taboo affair.

Today. Finally, today I can seize upon an opportunity. I know you're upstairs in your room getting dressed after your shower. Most of the family has headed to the beach. Only myself, you and a couple of aunts remain.

The aunts are deep in conversation, so I take the opportunity and sneak up the stairs to your room. I slowly and quietly open the door and see you standing in front of your mirror.

A part of me is disappointed you're already dressed. But it doesn't deter me. I know that soon your beautiful body will again be revealed to me.

I approach from behind and wrap my arms around you. I lean over your shoulder and lightly kiss your neck. I start at the base where it meets your shoulder, then work my way up toward that spot below your ear. My kisses gradually get more aggressive as I nip at you with my teeth and run my tongue along the most sensitive portions of your skin.

As your breathing starts to quicken, my hands begin to travel from your waist upward to your breasts. My fingers run up and over them, encasing them in my hands as I squeeze and knead them.

"I want you. I need you," I softly growl into your ear.

My hands slide back down. Moving toward the hem of your top. My left hand grabs the edge and lifts enough to slide underneath and run along your soft skin. The right hand continues lower to graze over the front of your pants. Just enough to let you know where I plan to spend time later.

My hands slide under your top purposefully driving toward your tits. Your shirt is tugged upward with my hands and I force the cups of your bra up and over your breasts, exposing your flesh for my hungry hands. All the while, my mouth has not left your body as I tease your skin with my lips, tongue and teeth. I leave your breasts long enough to unclasp your bra and tear the garments from your upper half.

I step back to look at your skin and the way your hair falls down your neck and onto your back. I run my fingers up your spine and through hair, then pull your head back so you're looking at me, but can still feel my ever-present hardon poking into your backside. I lean down and kiss you as hard as I can. It's clear my lustful animal instincts are taking over as I mash my face to yours, pushing my tongue into your mouth. One hand holds your head in place while the other moves back to your chest. I squeeze and knead your flesh while working toward your nipple. When my fingers close around your nipple I pinch it and roll it between my thumb and forefinger while pulling it away from the skin. Not enough to hurt, but enough to give you that jolt and let you know I am going to ravish every erogenous zone on your body.

My pawing travels across your chest to your left breast. I'm still kissing with a raw passion. Moving from deep open mouthed kisses to your neck and ears. My hand movements are sensuous yet rough with your tit. Kneading and pinching - begging you to moan and to vocalize that edge between pleasure and pain.

I spin you around and drop to my knees and take a breast in my mouth. I immediately suck as much of it into my mouth as I can. Then I release and focus on your nipple, working it over with my mouth.

My hands move quickly to your jeans, opening them and yanking them down to your knees. While mouthing your tits, I tease your pussy through the fabric of your panties. I alternate from gently tracing lines over your mound to squeezing the skin in my hand. I begin to forcefully trace my finger up and down your slit. Opening you up and feeling for the nub of your clit. My mouth begins its wet and sloppy descent from your chest to your waist. As my head nears your pelvis, my hands grab the waistband of your underwear and begin to pull them away from what I can tell is a wet and ready pussy.

I push you backward so you fall into the bed. In the same motion I'm tearing your pants from your legs. You lay there before me, completely nude. My eyes devour your body. Moving from your face, down over your breasts and to your glistening pink channel.

I waste no time diving back between your legs. My tongue runs a deep line from the bottom of your lips to the top, quickly finding your clit, flicking it and wrapping around it. I gently, but forcefully suck it into my mouth as I drive my middle finger inside you. I reach as far as I can while moving my hand in a circle.

Your hips buck toward me as I mouth your clit and fuck you with my finger. As I feel you open up, I add a second finger to the attack. This time, I ease my mouth off you and don't push as deep into you. I raise my head to watch your face as I push into you then curl my fingers up as I pull back. I gently place my left hand just above your mound. Adding a little more pressure as I work your G spot. I just keep reaching for that patch of flesh inside and dragging my fingers back. Over and over and over. As your breathing quickens and you continue to buck your hips against me, I hold the pressure and finger fuck you as hard as I can. I can feel your pussy flooding my hand with its wetness as you push toward an orgasm. I crawl up and suck on a nipple as I push you toward that point. And then your body tenses. I can feel you clinching around my fingers as you shudder from head to toe. You try to push me away, but I'm not done. Your body is mine.

I'm so turned on at this point, my erection almost hurts. I can feel my pants getting slick with the precum flowing from my cock. I know if I stood up, there's a good chance it would look like I wet myself.

I sit up and start fucking you again. This time I add a third finger. You can hear how wet you are as I piston in and out of you. I add a fourth, feeding my urge to fill you. I fold my thumb into my palm, enabling me to slide my entire hand inside you. I growl with delight and lust as I fill you up.

I love this moment. Knowing what I'm doing to you. I can feel every ridge and texture inside your pussy. I'm no longer fucking you with a wild ambition. I've slowed down. Both to allow you to get used to the pressure, but also for me to enjoy this moment and memorize all I can about what I feel inside you.

But then your body tenses again as another orgasm builds. I can tell it's too much as your muscles force me out of you and you push my hands away saying that you're too sensitive to be touched.

I climb back up to you and wrap my arms around you. This time I kiss you with a sweetness. "I love you," I say. I hold you tight letting you know that along with my insatiable animalistic lust for you, I also want give you the love and affection you need and deserve.

And in the back of my mind, I start thinking of what's next on our menu.

Broken Down on the Road (MILFs)

Two MILFs must pay for a ride.

*****

My name is Dave and I want to tell you an amazing story that happened to me last summer. Before I tell you what happened I'll tell you a little about myself.

I'm eighteen and just graduated from high school. This fall my plan is to go to the local community college to take classes to get my realtor license.

I'm little over six feet tall, and have an athletic build, but I'm no way any kind of jock. I've been told from time to time that I was handsome.

My Mom thought it would be great for me to work in her office so that I could see if I really wanted to be a realtor. My dad was all for me working this summer instead of just lying around. That's how I ended up working with my Mom.

Her boss (Mike) hired me and gave me all the odd jobs. I was the guy who put up the for sale signs, made the coffee and ran for the donuts. Of course I also was leaning a lot about being a realtor.

Mike had a very strict dress code. Not to go into the whole code I'll just keep it short, the women had to wear dresses or skirts and the men had to wear suits.

Since I didn't have my license I didn't have to wear a suit but had to wear slacks with a nice shirt. He also only had very fit people working for him. All the employees had gym memberships and worked out daily.

There was some kind of classes coming up to teach the new laws taking effect in a few months. The classes were the "teach the teacher" type of class. It's where only a few people would go and then come back to teach everyone else.

The classes were in a bigger town about four hours from us. Only three people could go. My Mom and one of the other females (Sue) were picked. Mike decided that it would be great idea if I went.

Mike told me, "Dave, I've picked you because I would like to see you continue working here while you attend school."

My Mom and Sue decided that we would head on up on a Saturday because they wanted to do some shopping on Sunday.

My Mom is 5'5", 130 pounds, with long blonde hair, hazel eyes. From working out every day she has well toned legs and a slim waist. From working with her I've noticed she has a gift for sales.

I'm sure glad Sue was picked I had certainly been noticing her around the office. She is short and very cute, the best way to describe her is a MILF.

When I was introduced to her she smiled and I thought she was so hot. Too bad she was married. From that day on I always sought her out just to ask her a question or two just so I could talk with her.

When she is around me she always flipping her short brown hair around in a way that is sexy as hell. I know she is doing this just to flirt with me. I try not to but whenever she is around I catch myself staring at her nice round tits and wondering what her bra size is. She caught me one day and just smiled at me.

We started our trip at 9 A.M. Since we we're traveling we decided to just wear jeans with a conformable top. My Mom was driving and she decided we would take the back roads instead of the interstate.

By taking the back road it took us away from all the towns. Being out in the middle of nowhere we had no cell phone service. The road was bumpingas no repair work has been done to it. I hadn't seen another car since we'd been on the road.

With no one on the deserted country road with us Mom was speeding. I was sitting in the back seat day dreaming when all of a sudden Sue yelled, "LOOK OUT!!"

I open my eyes to see a deer running out in the road. Mom swerved, missing the deer, but we ended up off the road. After checking making sure we were all ok Mom tried to move the car but it wouldn't move.

I got out of the car and walked around to see what was keeping us from moving. It appeared we hit a rock. "Oh shit, the front right wheel is busted!" I yelled.

Mom and Sue got out of the car and walked over to where I was. "Can you fix it?" Sue asked.

"No, the wheel is broken off the axle."

"Damn, we don't have any cell service out here either," Mom, added.

She continued, "The last town we went thru is about 15 miles behind us. I'm not sure how far it is to the next town."

Looking at the two women, I said, "Guess we will have to start walking."

"You are kidding, right?" Sue asked

"What, we're all in jeans and light tops on."

Mom was laughing now. "Yes, but Sue and I are in heels and walking is out, buster."

Knowing it was up to me to do something I said, "Guess I can start walking and see if I can find help."

"No, we're all going to stay with the car. Sooner or later someone will come by."

Here we were broken down on the highway and I was getting bored. So I was down looking at the wheel trying to see if I could fix it, when a van pulls up with four young men inside. All four of them got out of the van. "Looks like you all need some help."

As they walked around to where I was to check out the situation, I started to say something but my Mom spoke first. "Thank God you've turned up," she said," I didn't know what we were going to do."

All three guys looked at my Mom and ran their eyes up and down her. Then they noticed Sue standing on the other side of the car and checked her out.

That is when I decided to introduce us to them, hoping they would stop staring at the women. "I'm Dave and this is my Mom Mary. Over there is Sue."

"Whoa!" one of the guys yelled.

"That's got to be the best looking ass I've ever seen in a long time," another guy shouts.

"Heck, you're right, they both have a nice ass," someone added.

Not paying any attention to me the one close to me started talking. "So your name is Mary. I'm Brad, that's Jim, he's Gray and the dude over by Sue is Jake."

At least I knew they heard me when I introduced us. Mom answered, "Looks like the wheel is broken and we're hoping you could take us to the nearest town so we can get someone to fix the car?"

Brad then wandered closer to the front wheel bending down looking at it. "What seems to be the problem?"

"A deer jumped out in front of us and we swerved missing it, but hit that rock busting up the wheel. With no cell phone service out here we're kind of screwed," I replied.

"I say your screwed, looks like you're not going anywhere without a tow for sure."

Then looking at the other guys he looked at Mom. "How much money you three have? It's a long drive into town and we expect to be compensated forour time."

I jumped, looking at Mom and Sue. Being a little startled I checked my wallet as Mom and Sue were checking their purses. Then I walked over to the two women. We looked at each other putting what little money we had together.

Mom said, "We have a total of 50 dollars."

"That isn't enough," Brad stated smirking.

Sue looking at Brad and said, "When we get into town, take us by an ATM. and we will pay more."

Now laughing Brad looked at Sue. "I don't think so sweet heart. You'll pay up front or sit here until someone else comes by. Then again you can walk to town. I don't care."

He started to walk back to the van with the other guys following. Mom yells out, "Wait, maybe we can work something out."

Taking charged she looked at me then Sue and whispered, "Look, guys there is no way we're walking and we have already been here longer then I want to be. We need to make a deal with these guys. Dave, you get the luggage out of the car and Sue and I will talk with Brad."

Brad stopped and walked back towards Mom and Sue as I opened the trunk of the car to retrieve the luggage.

Gray walked over to me. "Hey, you need some help?"

"I'm not sure if they're going to make a deal, but if they do yes."

I couldn't make out what the other group was talking about. Then I saw Brad point at Gray then the van. Gray then said, "I think they might be coming close to a deal. Brad just pointed for us to move the luggage over to the van."

I said, "Cool," and we moved the three bags over to the van.

Gray picking up one suitcase, said, "We'll have to put them up on top in the luggage rack, so we'll have enough room for all of us in the van."

Just as we were putting the last suitcase on top of the van, I jumped. Mom's voice startled me. She was shouting, "I don't think so! We're not going to do that!"

Then Sue added, "No way!"

Then Mom added, "Look guys we both are married and that's my son. No, I can't, I just can't."

This statement made me wonder what they were they talking about. She didn't say she wouldn't, she just said she can't because I'm here. Now I'm thinking she would do what these guys wanted if I wasn't around.

Mom looked over at me and said, "Get the bags back down. This isn't going to work."

I looked at Gray. "What do you think that was all about?"

Gray replied with a smirk, "I'm sure he told them 'Cash, grass or ass, nobody rides for free,' and he won't change his mind."

As I got the bags off the van the guys were piling back into it. I saw Mom and Sue looking at me while in a deep conversation between each other. I picked up one suitcase and started to move it back to the car when Sue yelled, "WAIT Brad!! LET'S TALK!"

So I put the bag back down on the ground as the guys climbed out of the van again. This time Brad didn't have a friendly look on his face as all four of the guys walked over to Sue and my Mom. I also walked over to see what was going on.

With a mean but under control voice Brad said, "Ok, ladies, I hope you're not wasting any more of our time."

Mom started talking. "Look, guys, we've already been out here for a few hours and you're the only ones who have come by."

Then with a deep commanding voice Brad jumped in. "Look bitch you're wasting my time with a history class here." As he stared at her, he abruptly said, "Show us your titties."

"Excuse me? I told you we were not going to do that. We just want a ride and will pay you after we get to an ATM," Mom said angrily.

"I'm getting pissed. You're wasting my time. You want a ride you two will take off all of your clothes. I don't care if your son is here. If not, have afucking good time out here," he replied with no hint of compassion.

Then Jake added, "You want a ride then show them titties quick girls."

"You're breaking the law!" Sue forced out with a whisper..

"What law are we breaking? That's right, there is no goddamn law. I'm tired of your shit," Brad replied. He turned and started walking back to the van with the guys following.

"No wait, please, let us talk some more" Sue yelled out.

Dave turned and looked real mean at Sue, "Ok, don't take too long. We're not going to wait here all day!"

Sue grabbed my Mom and pulled her off to where no one could hear them talk. Everyone was watching them at this point. Sue was looking upset andwaving her hands around.

I knew both women didn't want to walk, but I wondered if they were going to be willing to submit to Brad's terms for a ride.

Now Mom was talking to Sue and they definitely were arguing with each other. They both looked over at me then back at each other as they talked. Mom looked upset but defeated and just shook her head up and down.

Brad shouted, "Goddamn you two bitches make up your minds!"

Sue then looked at him and said, "Ok, we'll do it but not here in the open."

Brad smirking now, "Well then where would you like to do it? I don't see anything but open space here."

"Over by the van where no one can see us from the road," Sue replied.

"Well, I see how busy this road is. Ok, move your asses over to the van."

Gray walked over to me. "Let's get that luggage back on top of the van."

With a concerned look on my face I picked up a suitcase. Gray, seeing my face, said, "Look, dude, don't try to be a hero. They'll just kick your ass. Just go with the flow. Anyway it looks like Sue and your mom are going along with it willingly."

"I'm cool," was the only thing I said. I didn't know if I would stay cool.

Gray and I had the first of the luggage on top of the van as the group was gathering around the side of the van. Mom and Sue were standing in the middle of the other three guys.

On one hand I was thinking this predicament is hilarious but in the other hand it wasn't, mainly because it was my Mom who was being forced. Guess she wasn't really being forced, but if we wanted a ride to town she had no choice but do a strip for these guys.

Brad said in a loud voice, "Okay, are you two happy now?" Then he continued, "I want both of you to tell us your full name and that you're doing this on your own free will. You first Mary."

Thinking this was odd I looked over at the group wondering why he would have them say this. As Mom was repeating what Brad wanted her to say I noticed it. Jim had a camera and was filming what was going on. I don't think Mom or Sue knew they were being filmed.

After Sue was done talking Brad commanded, "If you don't want to do this then don't. We don't mind leaving you here but if you want a ride then Mary you're first!"

I just finished handing Gray the second suitcase as Mom was looking around to see where I was. Guessing she was satisfied that I wasn't looking she started to unbutton her top.

Brad was talking very low to everyone in the group. I couldn't hear what was being said but everyone started to laugh even the women.

By the time we got the last suitcase on top of the van Mom had her blouse off. She didn't have a sexy bra on. It was still kind of sexy seeing her there in her jeans and white bra.

Now that Gray and I were done with the luggage we both moved over to the side of the van where the group was standing. I don't think either woman noticed us joining the group. Mom was looking around hoping they wouldn't make her go any further.

Then out of nowhere someone yells out, "Lose the bra you old bitch!!"

She slowly reached behind her and unclasped her bra. That is when I got this feeling of uneasiness.

Gray must of have noticed it and whispered into my ear, "Relax kid they're just your mom's tits, relax. Like I said before the guys will hurt you, so relax."

So I took a deep breath even though I still wasn't cool with the idea.

Then she reached up to her left shoulder pulling down her bra strap and letting it slide down her arm. Now holding on to the front of her bra she reached up and pulled down the other strap.

Now removing her hand where she was holding the bra she let it fall to the ground. The guys were cheering as they looked at her exposed mature boobs.

There was my Mom in her jeans with her boobs just hanging there fully exposed in front of these four strangers and me. One thing for sure a topless women in jeans is sexy as hell even if it is my Mom.

Bending down Brad picked up her bra, looking at it he yells out her bra size 34 C. As he tossed it into the van all the guys were making some kind of comment about her tits or bra size.

Brad looking at Mom ordered, "Ok, turn around so everyone gets a good look at them sexy mature titties."

She started turning around and as she faced the first guy shouted, "You have a great set there sweet heart!"

After that each guy made sure they commented on her tits. As she turned her boobs bounced and damn my cock was getting hard from watching my own mom's tits bounce.

When she finally faced me she had a look of surprise on her face. Then she just smiled at me as I checked her out. Her boobs sagged a little but they looked great. Her nipples were hard and pointing straight out. Her areolas were a nice light color.

Before she turned to the next guy I know she noticed I had a hard cock. As she turned towards Jim that is when she saw the camera pointing at her. In a nervous voice she whispered, "What, you're filming us?" She then quickly turned back facing Brad.

He was smiling while he looked at her. "Don't worry about it. We're documenting this in case you want to call the police. Remember we're not making you do this. It's your payment for a ride."

Mom was giving him a very evil eye. Sue was about to say something but didn't. They both knew it was better not to argue with him now. He was right they were doing this for a ride into town.

Since neither Sue nor Mom said anything else, Brad, still smiling ordered, "Now let's finish taking the rest off."

Mom started smiling again. I watched fascinated while she undid her belt. As she slowly unzipped her jeans she was looking around at all of us. I realized that I always wanted to see her naked and today it was happening.

Again as she moved, her tits were bouncing and I just couldn't take my eyes off them. Damn I wanted to drop my own jeans to play with my hard cock.

She pulled her pants down and I stared at her plain white panties. My eyes went to her crotch where the soft cloth covered her pussy. She kicked off her heels to get out of her jeans.

I couldn't help myself I was getting even more excited. Then slowly, she pulled the panties down and stepped back into her heels. Everyone was silent at the moment.

From where I stood I couldn't really see her pussy. I felt strange that I wanted to. I tried to move to get a good look, but couldn't without being noticeable. So I stayed where I was.

"Look at that ass, I told you all that ass was fine!" Jim yelled as he continued filming. Everyone laughed at that.

"You know what to do now," Brad added. With that Mom slowly tuned around again. As she faced me I got a great look at her cunt for the first time in my life. She had it trim, the only hair she had around her pussy was a landing strip. You couldn't help to see her large cunt lips between her legs as she turned.

After she was done turning Brad looked over at Sue. "Ok, it's now your turn."

Mom's slow strip had been sort of reluctant and she looked like she was embarrassed doing it. But now Sue looked like she was into it and was going to put on a show.

She pulled her top off and whirled it around over her head, grinning at the guys. I was really getting hard as I watched her.

She looked as if she enjoyed showing off. She grabbed the clasp on the front of her bra and hesitated, then suddenly dropping it as she shook her tits.She was a much bigger tease then my Mom and the guys were going crazy.

Brad then picked up her bra and announced, "36 D."

Someone yelled out, "Now there are some dam nice titties." Everyone else also shouted their approval.

Without being told she slowly turned making sure all the guys were getting to see her tits close up. I couldn't take my eyes off this sexy women as she bared her boobs in front of us. When she was finally facing me I noticed she had a big smile on her face, she even winked at me.

I think she was enjoying herself. I look at her tits and they were much firmer then Moms. Her dark areolas made her nipples look very long and they were still turned upward. She must have been very aroused as her nipples were hard as a rock.

After she finished her turn she slowly pulled down her jeans as she wiggled her ass. She didn't have a belt so they came down easy with just a little tug to get them past her hips.

She had on white panties also and she took them off slowly also. Making sure she removed one leg at a time from them. Her ass was much rounder than Mom's.

Again without being told she started to turn around. As her cunt came into view she was totally shaved.

To myself all I could say was, "Wow." She looked even better to me without her clothes on. There were even more cheers from the guys as they watched Sue turn around completely naked.

She even danced for a bit making sure we all got to see her ass and cunt. Her boobs were bouncing and we all simply watched taking in her beauty.

Brad made sure he had picked up all of their clothes and tossed them into the van. Here I was now looking at my Mom and her coworker standing nude in front of four strange men and me.

I was feeling sorry for them but I was also very excited about seeing these two MILFs being forced to stand nude for a ride. My cock was so very hard right then from watching them.

With both women standing outside of the van nude Brad, "Ok, you two, let's see you wiggle your asses now."

"What?" they both replied.

Smirking Brad said, "I said start wiggling them fine asses."

Mom and Sue slowly wiggled their butts. Now I was in heaven watching them shake their booty. This also made their boobs bounce around even more. All eyes were on them now. Jake had taken his cock out and was stroking it.

I turned my head to see if Jim was still filming what was going. Then all of a sudden I heard my Mom shriek.

I looked over to where she was to see Jake pushing her towards the open front door of the van. At that moment everything seemed to be in slow motion as I watched him shove her so that her hands were resting on the front seat.

Then he moved behind her and pushed his hard wood into her. The other three guys had their mouths open in surprise.

"Dam this old bitch is wet as hell. Don't worry Brad this slut wants a good fucking!" Jake yelled out.

Then I see Gray grabbing Sue and moving her towards the rear door of the van. He pushed her so she was in the same position as my Mom and he rams his Johnson into her cunt. "This one is also wet. Get in line guys we're going to have some fun now," Gray adds.

Here I'm pissed at what I just witnessed but excited at the same time. I moved towards my Mom to get Jake off her, but Brad grabbed me by the neck.

He threw me down to the ground. "Look dude those two women haven't protested, not once. So cool your jets or you're going to get hurt. Understand?"

I look at Brad then at my Mom. He was right they weren't complaining about what was going on. So I replied, "I'm cool."

Brad pulled me up as I watched Jake jack hammer his cock into my Mom. She started moaning, "Ohh, yes fuck me!" As soon as Sue heard Mom moaning she also started to moan, "Yes, yes, oh yes."

Jake was now pulling Moms head up by her hair as she was moaning from the pounding she was receiving.

As he held her head up he said, "You like this bitch? You love being used like a slut!"

All she did was moan a little louder. Jake then slaps her hard on the ass. "I asked you a question BITCH NOW ANSWER ME!!"

In between moans. "Yes...I...love being...used like this."

Jake then looked around for Jim and the camera. Finding him, now smiling looking right at the camera he shouts, "Damn, this one has one tight pussy!" He was fucking her even harder now.

He held onto Mom tightly as he pounded her hard with his cock for the next several minutes. This pushed her over the edge as she cried out into an intense orgasm while I watched.

Then I looked to where Gray was pounding Sue just as hard but he was shoving her face hard into the seat.

Jim was moving around making sure he was getting good shots of these two being fucked. He moved to the other side of the van and opened the door to make sure he had a good view of their faces.

Mom and Sue's boobs were bouncing all over the place as they were being fucked. As soon as Jake was done Brad replaced him. He was a little rougher then Jake. As he fucked Mom he grabbed her tits and was twisting them hard.

I'm not sure if she was yelling out with pain or pleasure, but she wasn't fighting him.

When Gray was done Jim put down the camera and got behind Sue. He grabbed hold of her nipples and pulled her tits as hard as he could as he fucked her.

As Jim was fucking Sue Jake grabbed her head to move her over to his cock. Before he pushed his cock into her mouth he said, "You like being used like a cheap whore."

Sue didn't reply so Jake slapped her face hard. She gave a little yelp and tried to pull her face away, but Jake held on to her and then slapped her again. Jim was smiling and enjoying the tough way Jake was treating Sue.

She finally replied, "Yes."

Then I turned to see what was going on with my Mom. Gray had moved her so she was outside of the van. He was face fucking her while Brad was fucking her hard from behind.

All of a sudden someone grabbed me and pushed towards Sue. Laughing Jake said, "It's your turn Dave."

So I didn't waste anytime in getting out of my clothes. Then I moved over to Sue and started planting soft kisses on her and then I kissed her on the mouth.

Then I said, "Since I met you I wanted to fuck you. I'm now going to fuck this pussy hard!"

Then my dick found her pussy and I pushed my cock into her waiting dripping pussy. As I entered her cunt I felt her cunt muscles clamped around my cock. I started fucking her with long fast strokes.

I was fucking her hard and didn't let up for one second. Sue was taking the pounding with ease. This made me drive cock even deeper and harder intoher swollen pussy.

Sue was now crying out, "Oh God! Oh God please fuck me hard."

"You are going to make me fucking cum!" I shouted out.

Several minutes later Sue cried out in a earth shattering orgasm. This pushed me over the edge as I began to cum hard and shot my load into her. As I pulled out I was pushed to the side to be replaced by another guy.

I went back to watching my Mom and after Gray was done I said to myself, "What the hell," and jumped in behind my Mom and started fucking her.

As I was giving her all I had Jim had picked the camera back up and said, "Look at this, he's fucking his own Mom." Everyone turned their heads to watch me fucking her.

Brad said, laughing, "That's it Dave, show your whore who is boss."

I stopped and started to think about what Brad just said while looking down at her. That's when I heard my Mom yell out, "Don't stop now!! Finish getting me off!"

So I went back pounding her with no mercy until I shot my load into her. I'm not sure if she had an orgasm or not, but then I didn't care either.

After a few hours we had all fucked both of the women a few times. When it was all done Brad said, "OK, you've paid for your ride plus. Let's get on the road."

As the guys grabbed their clothes to start dressing Sue yells out "Where's our clothes?"

Brad laughing "I'll give them back to you after we get into town."

Mom started to protest but before she could say a word Brad in a command voice "You will ride in the van nude or you can stay here nude. I don't care. We're not taking your luggage down and I'm not giving you your clothes back until we get into town."

Mom just looked at him, "You're an ass hole," as she and Sue got into the van. The rest of us also piled into the van. The next town wasn't very far.

As we pulled up to the grange Brad made Sue and Mom get out of the van nude. As I got out of the van he handed them their clothes and they got dressed as fast as they could. I don't think anyone but the guys in the van saw this.

As soon as the women were dressed the van pulled away and we walked into the garage so we could get someone to tow the car. Then we went and found a rental car and continued our way to the town where the classes were.

I will remember this day for the rest of my life.

Our First Experience with BDSM (BDSM)

Her bondage fantasy is played out.

I was at work and went to make a call on my cell phone when a photo memory popped up. It was a picture of my girlfriend, Sasha, from the Halloween party in Key West, called Fantasy Fest.

Fantasy Fest is a ten-day party in Key West, usually held during the last week of October. It is a place where adults gather and simply kick back not caring about the folks at home that are too inhibited to have a fun adult time. There are essentially no limits on what people wear for costumes. Some people will be covered in body paint from head to toe while others don't dress up at all. Many women are topless and others will wear their skimpiest lingerie. There is one woman who is there every year that takes a string and wraps it around her waist down her butt crack, and centered on her pussy. I would call this the ultimate G string. Everyone is here to have fun, if you were there and didn't have fun, you probably should have stayed home with those other inhibited people.

On the second night of this year's fest, we decided to dress up as Dom and sub. I was the Dom and Sasha was my sub. I wore black leather shorts that had a tare away pouch on the front with a leather vest to match.

We dressed Sasha up a little more extravagantly, after all, it is clearly all about the sexy ladies. We started with a heavy leather collar that was basically black but it had red trim and large loops for her leash. She wore black thigh high boots that laced up the back with a five -inch spike for a heal. This was complimented by a black leather body harness that went from the collar, circled around her 36C tits, leaving them completely exposed, and finished off as a very narrow thong that was only about an inch wide. Both of her nipples are pierced so she put some large jewelry on just to add a little bling.

She looked fucking hot; I clipped on her leash and told her she will do as she is told. She said, "Yes sir"

She reached for my dick only to find it very stiff and said, "I guess you like."

I said, "More than you can imagine, now let's go show you off." Once we were out on the street several people admired her outfit but as sexy as it was, she fit right in.

In real life, Sasha is a very respected partner at an international accounting firm. Her self-esteem is not an issue in any regard as she is confident in herself both professionally and in her personal life. Unfortunately, she needs to protect her identity when she is walking on the streets of Key West, nearly naked. Typically, she will get her picture taken hundreds of times and we expect she will appear on the internet but we don't need any of those shots showing up in the board room or maybe worse yet, the wash room. We found a black hood that has openings for her eye, mouth and nose. The challenge was to fund one that would not be too hot to wear all evening. We were successful in our search and the added mystery of her identity made it that much more interesting.

She is a beautiful woman, five foot six with a very pretty face, short black hair, gorgeous boobs, long shapely legs and an ass that completes the package. She is the type of women that as soon as you see her the first thing that comes to mind is, oh how I would like to do that.

I brought a riding crop with me because a common thing for the ladies to do is when two ladies dressed as subs meet, they will pose for pictures slapping each other on the ass. She asked what the crop was for and I told her "when you meet up with another lady who is going to smack your ass, give her the crop, it will make it more fun."

Sasha said, "For who, it will be me getting the sore ass."

I said, "Just try it and if it hurts, we will get rid of it." I smack her ass, she jumped but also smiled.

She said, "That wasn't bad, ok, it might be fun."

Anyway, back to the story, I texted the picture to her and she responded immediately with a happy face and commented," That was so much fun, can we do it again."

I responded, "Your assuming we are going to Fantasy Fest again this year."

"No, I meant, now," she followed with a happy face.

I said, "That would be fun but where were you planning to go."

She said replied, "How about the basement, we could call it the dungeon."

So now my dick jumped to attention and I can't begin to imagine what got into her.

I texted back, "We can talk about it, I have a conference call I have to be on."

She said, "Too bad, this was just starting to be fun. Luv U."

I got on my conference call and to be honest, I was having trouble concentrating thanks to my text conversation with Sasha. After about twenty minutes I got another text from

Sasha, this time it was a link to an adult web site's wish list. I opened it on my phone and found that she had made a wish list of bondage products. The first few items were simple things like handcuffs, ankle cuffs, flogs, ball gags and hoods. But then she got into some really funky stuff like a St. Andrews cross, a bondage fuck bench and other sex furniture. There was also some suspension equipment.

Needless to say, my concentration on my call was shot, I have no fucking idea what they were talking about.

Sasha and I had talked about doing some experimenting but clearly, we need to talk further.

I sent her a text, "Interesting, sounds like we have some things to talk about."

She responded, "☺ can't wait, see you tonight."

When I got home, she was already there. She greeted me at the door with a big hug and a kiss along with a cold beer. She said, "Can we go out on the deck and talk?"

I said, "Of course."

We sat down on the swing together and I said, "So you want to get cuffed and flogged."

She gave me a big smile and with no hesitation, she said, "Yes, I do." Clearly, she was excited, "I don't want to get beaten or hurt bad but a good spanking is a turn on."

I said, "I know we had some fun in KW with this but, what got you going today."

Sasha said, "I have been thinking about it and doing research ever since then." She continued, "You know when I had the flog in KW and I gave it to other girls in similar outfits and we playfully flogged each other."

I said, "Yah, and it was so sexy."

"Well", Sasha said, "Some of it was not so playful. A few of those girls whipped me pretty hard but you know I did the same to them."

Feeling puzzled, I said, "Where was I?"

She said, "A couple times you were right there and didn't realize what was going on and the best part was that I had two orgasms as a result of being whipped. One time, the other girl turned me sideways and had her fingers on my clit while she flogged me. It was the most intense orgasm I have ever had."

I said, "And I missed all this."

"My pussy was dripping the entire evening."

"Why didn't you tell me?"

She looked down and said, "I was a little embarrassed."

I asked, "So why are you telling me now?"

With confidence she said, "Because I can't get it off my mind and it was as exciting as hell. I'm ready to give it a try."

I said, "So you want to make a dungeon?"

"We can start out real small and expand if we like it." She said with enthusiasm.

We went downstairs to check out our new dungeon. Sasha said, "There is one thing that I really would like to have." She hesitated a bit and said, "A St. Andrews cross, it could go right there."

I was a little taken back by her boldness but said, "I have to admit, I really don't know what a St, Andrews cross is, can you describe it for me?"

Sasha explained, "It is a heavy wood cross that goes from floor almost to the ceiling. They can be straight up and down or some lean back, I think I want one that can be leaned back. They have shackles of some sort for each hand and ankle leaving the person standing spread eagle.

I said, "Interesting."

She went on, "The person that is bound to the cross can either face it or face away from it leaving the person vulnerable in different ways."

I said, "We could do that."

She smiled and said, "That's good because I already ordered it."

I said, "Without talking to me?"

She responded, "I figured we could send it back if you objected."

I said, "In the future you will discuss such large purchases with your master, understood?"

"Yes, sir"

We both knew we were teasing one another; the reality is that without batting an eye, she could afford to fit out an entire dungeon that would compete with 50 shades.

I sat down on a chair and told her, "Pull up her skirt and lay across my lap, you are going to get spanked for not talking to me first."

She said, "You are right, I should have talked to you first, please be gentle. Without hesitancy, her skirt was pulled up as far as it would go and her legs were spread wide with her ass in the air. She was wearing a white lace thong that looked sexy as hell when she was across my lap. Her pleasure was evident based on the damp spot that was clearly visible in the thin strip of fabric that hardly covered her pussy.

With that, I planted a firm slap right on her ass and she didn't flinch. After three more slaps, she was not moving but a I ran my hand over her thong covered pussy and it was now drenched. After a couple more slaps I could feel her legs spreading and she reached a finger right into her pussy. By now her ass was bright red, causing a wonderful contrast with her white thong. She continued pounding herself as if this might be her last orgasm ever, within moments she let go, causing her pussy to spray its juice in all directions.

She sat up with a couple tears in her eyes and I said, 'Didn't that hurt?"

She responded, "It hurt so fucking good. My ass is sore as hell but it is somehow connected to my pussy, that was one of the most electrifying orgasms I have ever had."

I asked, "When do you expect our cross to arrive?"

She said, "It will be about two weeks."

I said, "OK, you have an assignment. You are to find the toys that will make the cross fun."

She looked at me puzzled, "Not sure I know what you mean."

I said, "You will need to check out our current collection of toys and supplement anything we might be missing."

She said, "You mean stuff like ropes and handcuffs."

I responded, "Yah, pretty much but I also want to see a sexy outfit that is befitting of my sub, you are to please your master. I also want you to get something that I would not expect, surprise me."

Sasha said, "I can do that."

I said, "Sounds like a good time, now I need you to relieve the tension in my dick."

She said, "It would be my pleasure," as she unbuttoned my jeans and dropped them to the floor. She took my cock in her mouth sucking like the expert cock sucker she is. "I need you in me, please, fuck me, fuck me hard."

I did as she requested pulling her wet thong to one side driving my cock into her fast and hard. Her orgasm was almost immediate and mine followed quickly. She put the thin strip of fabric back over her cunt saying, "That will hold some of it in, I want to feel you juice all evening."

While we were waiting for our cross to arrive neither of us said anything about it. I was kinda wondering if this was something she really wanted or if it was just a passing fantasy that passed after a spanking and a good orgasm. We have always enjoyed a little rough sex but this would be taking it to a new level that neither of us has much experience with.

Finally, on Thursday afternoon, when I got home there was a note on the table. It said, "It's here and I hope you are ready for some fun. If you would like, go upstairs and take a shower, you will find a gift for you on the bed but don't open until after your shower."

I went upstairs and saw a package on the bed and a cold beer sitting in ice on the dresser. I cracked the beer and headed to the shower.

When I came out of the shower, I opened the package, I found a pair of black jeans, mesh thong and sneakers. Under them there was a black hood a paddle and a magic wand. I had to snicker about the magic wand as we wore out the last one. Finally, there was an envelope, when I opened it there were ten pictures of Sasha secured to a St. Andrews cross in our basement. Half of the pictures had her dressed in some very sexy outfits and the balance of the shots had her totally naked. Obviously, she has been working at this and she had some help.

There was a note, it said, "HI Babe, Oh, please forgive me, tonight I must call you Sir. Obviously, you were not expecting this tonight, Surprise!! As you can see, I have been very busy. We can thank my friend Sarina for helping set things up and taking the pictures, I will explain later. It is my hope that you will get as much pleasure out of my fantasy as I expect I will. Whenever you are ready, I'm downstairs secured to the cross waiting for you. I cannot get free; I am at your mercy. It is my hope that you will rip my clothes to shreds than use this paddle on my bottom until it is hot. I hope you will drag the twitch across my pussy until it drips. Feel free to wear the outfit I got for you but only if it is your desire. All my love, Sash."

I thought about leaving her bound for a while on her own but I am afraid my dick might explode with anticipation. I put the mesh thong and the jeans on and got the hood she wore in Key West. I grabbed the paddle and headed down to our new dungeon. Just before going down the stairs I got another beer and slipped the hood on. I was not crazy about wearing the hood but I really wanted this experience to be everything Sasha was hoping for. The hood had eye and mouth openings but it would be nearly impossible to know who was wearing it.

When I got to the bottom of the stairs there was my beautiful Sasha, bound facing the cross with her lovely round ass in a vulnerable position. Both hands and feet were held with heavy leather cuffs and there was a collar around her neck. I was a little surprised that she was not clad in a leather harnesses or other more traditional BDSM type outfit. Instead, she had an old worn out cotton t-shirt and shorts on. The t-shirt was old and warn thin allowing her nipple rings to poke nearly through the fabric. The shorts were also very old and worn but they were also one or maybe two sizes to small which forced her ass cheeks to push out.

I chose to not say a word. I wanted to be her unknown aggressor. I wanted her to wonder what my next move would be. I wanted her to wonder, maybe it was not me under that hood. I wanted her to be careful about what she wished for now that she in a totally defenseless position.

I looked around the room and indeed saw she had been busy. Our camera was set up on a tripod at about a 45-degree angle from where she was bound. She always loved getting her picture taken, generally in lingerie but hardly ever nude. Tonight, would be different, she will be nude.

There was various paraphernalia around the room, her new magic wand was plugged in and ready to go but there was also a harness for the wand, hmm, interesting, not sure about that one. There was a variety of flogs, twitches and small whips. It was all very interesting but I also had a little surprise for her.

I walked up to her and pulled a blindfold out of my pocket. She saw it and said, "I would rather be able to see."

I started to put the blindfold on her and got a bit of half-hearted resistance. Starting at the back of her head, I used the edge of the paddle to slowly trace down her neck and back, finally making its way to her ass. With one smooth motion, I struck her exposed ass cheek which caused her to jump. Now, she chose to not resist getting her blindfold.

I sat down in the overstuffed chair that was right behind her and enjoyed my beer making just enough noise for her to know I was still there but not have a clue as to what I was up to. While I was sitting, I figured out what the leather harness was for, it went around her waist and hung down to hold her magic wand in place for effortless pleasure. When I finished my beer, I quietly went up behind her and started touching her very gently at first but increased the pressure as I went.

I spent time kissing and licking her neck and backs of her ears while squeezing her tits through her t-shirt. She was squirming now with nearly every touch when she said, "Please, rip my clothes off."

I continued teasing her without tearing her clothes off as she requested in her letter. I did however wrap the harness around her waist and attached her magic wand applying pressure on her still covered pussy. When I turned it on, she smiled and said, "My favorite toy, thank you."

As is always the case with the magic wand, she had her first orgasm in only minutes and they just kept coming. After about the fourth one, her shorts were soaked and pussy juice was running down her legs. While in the midst of an orgasm she was trying to say, "Enough, please turn it off, turn it off, of fuck its going to come again," and I turned it off. She said, "Oh fuck, why did you turn it off?"

With that, I turned it back on. After her next orgasm she begged, "I'm done, I can't take any more, please turn it off. Oh fuck, its coming again." And that was followed by yet another orgasm. "Fuck, please turn the fucking thing off, please." I turned it off after at least ten orgasms.

She just went quiet as she was leaning against the cross. I let her rest for about ten minutes while I had another beer.

I walked over behind her and touched her back with my hands. She said, "What are you going to do. Fuck you, talk to me, what the fuck are you going to do?"

I put both hands on her t-shirt and in one motion ripped the back open. The bare flesh of her back was exposed and she looked so fucking hot bound to the cross and looking like she was getting rapped. I took the riding crop and traced lines up and down her back than eventually cracked it on her pale white skin leaving a red mark. I continued this teasing and smacking process for several minutes each time smacking a little harder.

Sasha said, "Hey asshole, is that all you got?"

I guess this was supposed to anger me but it only got me more excited. I grabbed one leg on her shorts, in one steady motion they resembled a loin cloth rather than a pair of shorts. Her ass and pussy were now exposed.

I stood behind her in silence for a minute or two then, without any warning cracked the paddle on her white ass cheek. She jumped and with a cracking voice said, "Come on you fucking dick, paddle me like you mean it, I want my ass to feel the electricity go through me."

I was so tempted to paddle her hard but I of course didn't want to really hurt her. So instead I used moderate strength but I paddled her, maybe as many as twenty times.

With incredible enthusiasm, she said, "Fucking me, now you got it you fucking pussy."

I dropped the paddle and stripped my clothes off. My dick was so fucking hard I was afraid it was going to cum without getting touched. I pulled her hips toward me and slid my cock right in her slippery cunt.

I could not hold on, as soon as I bottomed out, I was filling her with my cum. I continued pumping as hard as I could and in no time, she said, "Oh fuck, I'm going to cum again." She had her most intense orgasm of the night that included squirting pussy cum al over the floor.

I sat back down in the chair and realized we never took any pictures. I took the opportunity to get a bunch of shots of her in her most used state. She looked like a slut that had been used by anyone that wanted some. Actually, she was sexy as hell standing there spread eagle with sperm dripping out of her.

At this point she was exhausted and it was time to let her go. I continued not saying a word as I put my thong and jeans back on. I went over to her and unhooked one ankle strap and one wrist strap but I held her hand in place sending the message that she was not to move. I turned away and walked up the stairs. When I got to the top, I removed my hood and through it down to her.

I went up to the living room and turned the TV on. When I heard her come through the door I said, "Hey Babe, would you grab me a beer?"

She responded, "No problem babe, I'll be right there."

Sasha came into the living room wearing a white thong and cami top. She made it a point of making sure I saw the contrast or red to white on her ass as she handed me my beer.

I asked, "Why is your ass so red?"

She smiled big and said, "Because my wonderful boyfriend just let me live out one of my fantasy."

I asked, "Was it fun?"

"Like you can't believe." She replied

I said," Did you get any pictures?"

She said, "Unfortunately only a few which I did get to take a quick look at, they were hot, it really is too bad he didn't get more."

I said, "Pictures would have been fun, sorry I will not get to see many. Do you think it might happen again? At least that way you could get more pictures."

Sasha responded, "Oh, I assure you it is going to happen again." And she went on to say, "Hey babe, would you mind if I sucked your dick?"

I said, "Please do, that would be nice."

The Games Some Daughters will Play (Forbidden)

Before school tussle leads to night of "adult entertainment".

*****

Aged eighteen and one day, Kylie was wondering what she could do now, that she couldn't before. It just seemed so anti-climactic. So she downloaded a new browser to her computer and linked it to a new g-mail. Then she started typing the craziest shit into Google—most of it disgusting, some of it literally shit. The only taboo with a good mix of naughty and funny was incest. From the photos with laughable captions and forums for "serious" discussion, a world of entertainment awaited. It took her no time to conclude the confessions were plainly made up. They were all too over the top. It would be even more furtive, she thought, adding a comment that someone with a brain could believe.

d/F: I'm eighteen and have been masturbating thinking of about my father and I feel very ashamed about the feelings I have, but they're very real so please refrain for judging too harshly. So look, I don't want to spoil my relationship with him by making advances, and I don't think I want real sexual relations. I'm just wondering if anyone has advice on how I can enjoy a little more "contact". Now I'm older I think the old tickle fights and wrestles I used to have with him when I was a kid would have a new dimension. He does it still with my little sister but it would be strange if I tried to join in. So I'm asking if people here have suggestions about fun and games stuff we could do that would not jeopardize normal relations going into the future.

She hit post, satisfied her inquiry sounded more genuine than anything on there. For the real sex fiends, there was always the dark web. She knew she was safe to browse while she used plain old Safari so toddled along to places where people post captions over short clips. Most started, "I like it when Daddy..." or, "Don't you love when your step-daughter..." then followed on with something naughty and funny that put a new spin on an ordinary fuck scene.

She had obviously struck a chord on the forum because when she returned there were already comments. She wondered why some people even came on this forum if all they were going to say is "don't play with fire". They were probably Christians and prime offenders. There was one she liked though:

If your father is still playing physical games with your younger sibling, then this is your "in". All younger siblings dream of their older siblings playing with them more, and all fathers are happy to see the younger ones getting the attention from their older sibling. If you join in next time they're playing no one will suspect your ulterior motive.

In response to that comment was this piece of advice:

Since your father raised you, he still thinks you're totally innocent. So, if you accidentally touched his dick, or wore a nightie without any panties, you would get even more contact without being suspected. Also, what makes you think he wouldn't enjoy some sexy games too? I've got an eighteen year old daughter at home and I would blow my wad if she was like you. Keep it all disguised as a game and enjoy your last years at home.

Ben's older daughter was far too mature for rough-house dad games nowadays. Makeup and shopping are serious business. The last thing she would be a part of were horsy rides like the ones Natalie, her younger sister, demanded each night after dinner. Ben was on his hands and knees while Natalie sat like a cowboy on his back. She dug her heels into his stomach to keep herself straight and then giggled and yelped as he couriered her from the dining chair to the sofa without her feet being allowed to brush the carpet. To her it was something about dolls getting to safety.

All he saw of Kylie when she crossed the room were her legs.

"Kylie, could you pass me Barbie?" Natalie asked her, wasting her breath.

Nat and Ben had a little song for such times: "Kylie's too big to have fun." It seemed like water off a duck's back to Kylie, but it did make Natalie feel a bit better about being ignored. It was that time of the night when Kylie got slices of cucumber to put over her eyes.

Horsey loped on back to the sofa, singing his song. "Kylie's too big to have fun, dum dum dum dum dum, Kylie's too big to have fun...". Ben had forgotten that it was for sour pus Kylie over there in the kitchen that he started singing this song and was now just hooked by the tune.

"Alright, get off," he heard Kylie say. "It's my turn. What's the game?"

Natalie told her that you have to get dolls from the dining chair to the sofa.

"Oh god, she's heavy! You'll have to sit back more." It was not that a hundred and twenty pounds was actually heavy. For a girl her height she was a waif. It was just that her weight, in the saddle of his back, came as a jolt.

Horsey started to shuffle. "You better hold on."

"Where do I hold?"

Eager to help her big sister Natalie guided Kylie's legs around Ben's muscular torso. But there was a problem. She had longer legs. Her heels didn't dig into his tummy. They landed right in his crotch. Ben repositioned them with his hand but they fell right back in the only place they could go. She had to grip firmly to stay on board and not let her feet touch the carpet.

Ben knew he really shouldn't be reading some of the filth he had been reading online. But with free speech and forums, it seemed the world was obsessed by taboos. How many of the "confessions" were real though? He doubted most would be. He told himself to lighten up and just have some fun. His wife would be the ultimate beneficiary if this little game made him horny. He might actually have a reason to fuck her.

So off they went. Ben sang "Kylie's too big to have fun," because it was still in his head and he really had to keep everything light. His cock was getting pummeled back there.

Her hands on his bare lateral muscles were equally welcome. He had to go shirtless when playing this game so the cowboys could get a skin-on-skin grip.

After one run Kylie put her feet on the floor and said, "There, easy. No more saying I'm too big to have fun."

"Hang on," Ben said. "Spend some more time with your sister."

"I've got my cucumber, see ya."

Funny, he thought, how she always needed the whole of the cucumber, not just the slices she took from the end. She was too young, surely, to fit cucumber in her?

She was half way to her room when he had an idea. She was wearing an almost see-through nightie with no evidence of underwear indentations across her firm little bottom. And Ben knew Natalie would enjoy some more Kylie time too.

"How about we add a little incentive? You two take it in turns, and each time you make it across, there and back, I'll pay you a dollar."

Natalie couldn't believe it.

Kylie said, "How about two dollars?"

"Alright. Two dollars."

"Oh kewl! I'm first."

Natalie didn't complain. Anything to keep her sister there playing.

This time her new enthusiasm made Kylie a little more careless with the way she straddled Ben's back. As his cock felt the welcome pressure of her heels, his back felt the scrape of her stubble and something fleshy a tad further back. Those weren't her flaps, surely?

Did she know what she was doing? She must have. She had had a boyfriend and Ben assumed they had done some petting. He knew too that with their internet access her generation all rushed straight to the most laughable filth: possibly the same stories and notice boards he read to get off. He knew he really should stop with all that now Kylie was of legal age. There was too much temptation. He might do something stupid. But maybe the seed of temptation had already been planted?

Still, she was on his back now. Why not enjoy it!

Ben dropped his head and loped along like an old worn out donkey, too burdened to sing. It was not up to him now to gee the girls up. His money would keep the game going. A half decent hooker would have cost him a hundred trips back and forth, and there was no way the game would go that long. He knew that for Kylie the hourly rate was better than she got at McDonalds. For Natalie it would be like Christmas mid year.

When Kylie alighted from her third ride Ben checked his lower back with his finger. There was a wet patch. While she wasn't looking he had a quick whiff of his fingers. They smelt like her bunny hole. Not any bunny hole. Kylie's bunny hole. Like any man he knew the smell of his teen daughter's bunny hole from her underpants left in the bathroom.

Natalie was so much lighter that her turns took just a few seconds.

"Make sure you keep track of the money I owe you. Oh no, here comes the heavy one."

Once again he dropped his sad donkey head. But this time she put herself into the butterfly pose, with his shaft as the meat in her foot sandwich.

"Are you r-right there?" he asked.

"Just getting settled."

"Got a good grip?"

People didn't used to talk about incest when he was her age. They didn't have the same entertainment on the internet or confessional forums to turn to. There just came a time when every young adult was invited by someone very inappropriate for fondue with fluffy ducks. When Ben was eighteen it was an aunty he stayed with who melted some cheese after midnight then came to his room to invite him to play. Fond memories of that evening, also on a living room floor, drifted through my mind as he waddled back and forth with Kylie's naked clit on his back.

The night cost him thirty-two-dollars and some back pain the next day, but it was like a night at a strip club at home-cooking prices. Fantastic. He had the right cash in his wallet to pay on the spot.

"Yes Natalie," he assured her, "that's in addition to your pocket money on Friday, so don't tell your mother."

He resolved to keep lots of small denominations on hand at all times.

"So, do I get a big hug for being the world's most awesome-est dad?"

He sure did! Natalie showed by example how to crush the air from a chest.

"Come on, like your sister," he told Kylie when it was her turn.

There was some extra tenderness though. The hug came with a deep sigh and a nestle. She had been without a boyfriend for months and he felt her telling him so in her hug and parting kiss on the lips—not where kisses should land from a daughter.

As Ben watched her pitter patter back to her room, with twelve dollars in hand and a slimy vagina, he pondered what new knowledge she was taking to her cell of cucumbers. Even though it had only been through her feet, she now knew the thickness and length of his member. He hoped she would one day find a nice husband whose dick was just a bit smaller.

Sitting with a beer before bed, Ben resolved not to look at anything online for a month. Let fondue nights be of the eighties, and whatever happened in the old days to make it okay, belong to times when they all were peasants.

Ben thought it was right for society to crack down on incest. For those who transgress—not with their own age group, but the next generation—he had no doubt the sex was like base jumping compared to ground sports. But a lot of the rush would come from it being forbidden. Cocaine can have that allure, but it would soon lose its shine if you were addicted. Lifting the taboo on daughters would increase the incidence but lower the thrill, the first bad for society, the second a loss for the brave.

"Which of those two kinds of people am I going to be?" he wondered, on his third beer.

Ben was so proud of his girls. Both had gotten themselves up and ready with a half hour to spare before he had to drive them to school. Kylie's fair skin still glowed from the shower, dusted with the lightest touch of fine makeup. Her blonde hair was tightly drawn back in a pony tail.

With his wife left for a conference that morning Ben would have today and the next with no one looking over his shoulder. Unless his wife had set cameras he wasn't aware of (and the woman instilled paranoia) he could let his eyes fall on Kylie's grey private school tunic, the slender thighs between its hem and her long socks. Even the polished black private school shoes were a bit of a turn on.

He broke his stare to pour himself some more coffee. By the time he returned Kylie and Natalie were engaged in a play fight. He had no idea how it had started but was excited by the prospect of more panty flashes. His wife had a policy of buying only white cotton, even for Kylie, and throwing them away at the first sign of staining.

"Keep it on the floor!" he said sternly, not only for a better view of Kylie's tight butt, but so they wouldn't crash into a window if they got too exited.

Momentarily Kylie had her sister down for the count.

"One... Two..."

"Daddy," Natalie cried and threw one hand out toward him. "Tag team. Tag team."

Natalie's face was being swept by Kylie's shampoo scented hair. Trading places presented an opportunity to make any man jealous. He was, after all, sharing a house with a 10.

When he tagged Nat's hand Kylie released her, leapt to her knees and squared up for fierce battle.

"Oh dear, look at that warrior face!" Ben said.

"I'm bigger since the last time you tried this," she warned him and lashed with her red nails like a cat.

"Now just go easy," he said, afraid of the mischievousness in her eyes.

It started with hand slaps until she got hold of his wrists and put nail marks in each. The only escape was to prize her hands off and embrace her in a chest-to-chest hug. The white lacy bra under her school shirt had pushed her breasts into the shape of round apples.

Ben made sure to keep their battle close to the carpet. Despite the vastness of their living room they still could knock over a speaker.

But the thing about keeping wrestling safe is you really only have two positions: laying over your opponent when she is face down, and face-up once you have turned her over and are pinning her shoulders on the floor for the count.

Her thin arms had speed but no power, just like her thin torso. All of her goodness could be laid out as if for dissection, or just penetration, even if it did mean using his dick as a cattle-prod on her pubis and smearing her breasts with his chest. He was about to start counting to three but was struck by her teeth. They were always so perfectly white and framed by those striated lips. He would just have to look at them and slide back and forth so the cap of his dick pressed her pubis, and he would come.

Her teeth reminded him of a common cause for leaving late in the morning. "Natalie, have you brushed your teeth?"

"Oh whoops!"

"Go on, get in there and make sure you set the timer for three whole minutes."

She raced off and left Ben all alone with his hot older daughter pinned on the floor by his cock.

"You don't want to know how we played this game when we were younger," he said, looking down over her lightly made face.

"Let me guess. Catch and kiss?" She made the sarcastic face of a girl with nothing left to learn from adults. He may as well leave.

"Oh you posh private school girls," he sneered. "You've never heard of finger-wrestling, I bet?"

"Thumb wrestling?"

"Finger-wrestling. It's full body wrestling but the loser gets fingered."

"That doesn't sound very hygienic!"

"Well aren't you lucky times are so soft! Am I meant to be counting?"

She tried shaking him off as though her three seconds had passed but Ben pushed her down casting a flash of fear in her eyes.

"Are you kidding me?" she asked. "Is that what you did?"

"Finger wrestling? It was the thing."

Then her eyes narrowed and Ben could see she was thinking. "How far would the fingers go in?"

"Hardly at all."

A considered look turned her head sideways with her eyes still on his.

"What?" he asked. "Do you want me to show you?"

"It's just a game. Right?"

"Alright princess. I'll finger you then."

Not wanting to rumple her uniform—one of his jobs in the house was the ironing—he undid the top button and came from above. She poked out and twisted her tummy and made a grimacing sound, but that's what all the girls used to do when playing this game. It was no fun without some resistance.

"Wait until I tell all my friends I got fingered by you!"

"Life isn't fun without a few secrets. A bit gooey there Kylie. You been thinking bad thoughts?"

She said nothing.

The last time he played this was at a Christian youth camp. He was more brutal then than he would ever be with his daughter. He just circled her slippery clit the best way he could to make it feel nice.

"It's just another kind of massage," he said in a low soothing tone.

"How long did this game used to go for?" she asked with a sigh.

"How long did I tell your sister to brush her teeth for?"

"We've maybe got another two minutes. It's okay. I'm not going to tell."

Emboldened by her rapid response he asked her if she wanted to double the fun and make it a game of catch and kiss too.

She didn't reply. She just reached for his mouth with those thick crinkly lips. He pressed his mouth against hers and was engaged in youth disco pash. Those were the days when he would just dive into the snake pit of tongues and girls' spit. Keeping it going past the end of the song meant going steady, so he would never do that. Better to keep on rotating and try to get to every hot one with the same attitude as your own.

"Hmm, hmmm, Kylie, you're so... delicious," he murmured.

"You're pretty good too."

He gazed into her lightly done eyes. "Oh gosh," he said, then dived back on in. There was chemistry there. The idea seemed absurd, of her and him gelling.

"Alright, that's a rabbit hole we're going to fall into if we don't break it up."

"Rabbit hole?" she asked, puzzled. The pet word in their household for a vagina was bunny hole.

He hastened to correct any assumptions. "Like Alice in Wonderland. There's a line when it stops being a game. So it's good we didn't cross it—you cutie."

He dropped her at school and watched her bounce off to join her upper class friends. Seeing she was plainly the best of the best gave Ben a strange satisfaction. It was his finger massaging that one's bunny hole less than a half hour beforehand.

He knew he had to go further. She had the best legs and butt of any of those girls. Quite a few were too hefty. They had overworked parents who feed them all crap. Ben's girls had a home husband in charge of planned meals. He was responsible for creating the healthiest specimen in one of the city's most privileged schools. He deserved the first fruits of his labors.

Cars were honking.

"What's up? Oh shit, sorry!"

He had been stopped in the quick drop-off zone. He had an erection in front of a school. His life was in a kind of a slide.

There was a spot under the stage of the school hall where Kylie could wag her first class and browse the web on her phone. She went straight to her thread.

I must say, you both know a lot about incest. I'm typing at school so I'll have to be brief. I did the horsey ride thing with no underpants. I felt a bit in over my head because where my feet had to go meant I was pressing them on my father's dick. And it got very hard. And my bits were skin to skin on his back and I know I left slime there. So then this morning, I tried wrestling with my sister and we did the tag team thing where he took her place. When she was out of the room he said he was going to show me what finger-wrestling is. It's apparently a game from when he was younger. Basically, it meant him fingering me at the same time as we played catch-n-kiss. He broke it off and said there's a line when it all stops being a game. He says we haven't crossed that, which is is awesome. So what I'm asking, I guess, is if anyone knows some more games?

At lunch time she sat on the toilet and checked her thread there. There was just one reply.

Try putting on a play with your sister. Or a talent competition. Then when your sister's in bed tell him you want to give him a fashion parade. It's pretty simple. You just wear less and less each time you come out. His eyes burning into your body will be at least as exciting as him putting his finger in your vagina.

When Ben set the dinner table he made a point of putting Kylie's plate in front of her mom's regular chair.

"Can you pass my plate down?" Kylie asked.

"I want to make you the lady of the house while your mom is away."

Kylie looked two inches taller as she walked around the table to take the prime spot.

Natalie said, "Daddy, Kylie and me are going to do a play for you after dinner. We've been planning it. So you have to make time to watch."

Ben finished packing the dishwasher and went to see what they had done to the living room. They had the mic stand, kid-size plastic furniture for the props and the flute neither of them had learned to play. Sweet though, was the bowl of Doritos and six pack of beer set especially for him by the sofa.

"I won't drink that much you sillies!"

"We want you to enjoy yourself," Kylie said. "Mom's away and it's always about what she wants. So we've got it all planned so it's all about you."

It was hard to imagine how amateurish performances scripted since they got home from school would be better than a night in his room just looking at porn, but it was his best beer they had brought from his man cave and he had a front row seat on his forbidden obsession.

They started with piss-poor dances "choreographed" to songs by Nirvana, the only band they knew he enjoyed. Kurt Cobain would roll in his grave. Then came the readings from On The Road. Blasphemy!

After three beers he made himself a part of the act by gazing at Kylie to see when she'd blush. When she did, she said, "I'm hot, I've got to go and get changed." She came back minus the jeans in her much cooler nightie.

The play was atrocious and a ventriloquist would mine pop songs with more expression. But none of that mattered with Kylie's little funyums giggling inside of that nightie.

Finally nine o'clock came around and Ben could say it was Natalie's bed time and that he would look forward to next year's royal gala amusements.

When Ben had been reading Natalie her story he had assumed Kylie would be retiring with a cucumber, not putting on the late evening makeup and erotic attire that she was wearing when he returned. She had slunk into the jumpsuit he'd once bought her so she could go trick-or-treating as Cat Woman from the movie Dark Night. She still had the mask, the boots, the ears—the whole costume. She must have worn something under it for Halloween though because this time the outline of her box flaps and puffies were unbearably clear. She held one of his beers in her hand, three quarters empty.

"What, there's another performance?" he asked.

"The mature audiences part," she said and scratched the air with a hiss. "Sit down. I've memorized the whole fight scene."

It began with a minute of high kicks, cartwheels and punches.

"Say 'No Killing'," she told him.

Ben said, "No Killing."

"How boring!"

It seemed she knew the whole movie by heart.

"What's this bit?" he asked when she climbed on the arm of the sofa beside him.

"It's where I jump from the roof," and she theatrically stepped cautiously and sat close beside him. Her painted lips came right to his face. "My mother told me never to get into cars with strange men," she said breathily, then stood to take her applause.

"Bravo! Kylie, that was amazing!"

"Oh thank you! Can I have some more beer for my courage?"

"Sure. Why courage?"

"My next act comes with a nudity warning."

Her hands were fumbling badly with the bottle and opener.

"Kylie," Ben said, taking the beer to do the job for her. "You can relax without getting drunk. Look, it's just me. Your boring old father."

"I'm going to make a fool out of myself aren't I?" Out came the bottom lip and she looked ready to sob.

"Not at all. If this night's for me, as you say, then female nudity has to be on the menu, somehow. It's probably the only thing in the world that I find amusing." It was his own nervousness on display now.

"If you laugh I'll never forgive you."

He clasped her trembling hands to steady his own and kissed his girl on the forehead. Everything about this was wrong. His erection. His burning desire to see her disrobed. But there was a thread there that might just hold all the weight, and that was the idea that nothing was real. It was just a performance or game. "Kylie, I'm with you. And home is a smart place to explore aspects of your sexuality where you can't get embarrassed."

He hadn't kissed her full on the lips since that morning and would have done so right then, if there was some way to say it was a game.

"I don't know what you can possibly go and get changed into that's sexier than you as cat woman, but kid, you've got me as horny as hell and I want to find out."

She immerged in white heels, white stockings and matching diaphanous panties with pubes showing over the gusset. The star though was the white feather boa she had recently bought for a Great Gatsby party. It was the only thing that covered her chest.

Ben had decided while she was changing to behave as he would in a strip club. He didn't go to those places to talk to the girls. He went there to stare—to be a creep. That was the kind of daddy his baby said she was here to amuse. He couldn't be somebody else.

She set the TV to play "Bang Bang" from The Great Gatsby soundtrack. With her back to Ben and her face to the screen she tried to learn the moves on the spot, happily shuffling a half beat behind.

Ben had seen strippers in their twenties with figures as tight, and strippers as young as eighteen, but had never seen youth and fitness in the same person. Her musculature and waist line didn't come from the gym or pole dancing. It was from good breeding and posh school activities like horse riding and skiing.

152

It was the feebleness though that was driving him crazy. What was it with strippers that they thought men would want them to look powerful and in control?

She had found her rhythm, if not the right dance steps and was daring to let the boa away from her breasts. Leaning sideways for a view of more side boob would be like scrutinizing a learner magician, so he stayed where he was. All he did, and there was no way he could help this, was slide lower down on the sofa. Contracting his ass and raising his hips was rubbing the tip of his rod against the inside of his trousers.

The song ended and she turned to face him, the boa held tight to her chest.

"I'm sorry, I bet that wasn't sexy at all."

"I don't know about sexy, but it was fucking arousing."

"Really?"

"I'm going out of my mind."

"Really?"

"I don't know what we're going to do now though." If he gave her an easy out she would go put on some clothes. "Do you want to sit with me for bit?"

"What for?"

Of course she would ask that. A know-it-all teenager can't sit with her old foggy dad unless there's a reason. Ben had to think fast. Then he realized: this was an evening of entertainment while mom was away. He had to keep playing that line.

"Oh I don't know," he said. "In those strip clubs the girls sit with the men between songs. They get money for selling them overpriced drinks."

"Okay."

He reached out his arm and she slid close beside him. Though she was sheathing herself with her feathers there was still a lot of skin to admire. He held her tight to keep her face close.

"Now you've got to be over-the-top flirty," he told her.

"Oh hi there, I'm Kylie," she said with a pat.

"Hi Kylie, I'm Ben." He began slowing stroking her arm.

"Have you been enjoying the evening?" she asked, running her nails down the stubble that grew on his neck.

"Well the G-rated stuff wasn't really my thing. But your dance just then was amazing."

"Oh thank e-yew. You're a big sweetie then aren't you!" She planted a kiss on his cheek.

"So are you Kylie. Do you mind?" He was pulling her boa, slowly, without objection, over her shoulder. He ground his teeth in defiance, knowing he was joining less than one percent of all man who receive justice. Most never see a breast their sperm has created.

There are things every pervert looks for in a teen gland. An upward inclination of a puffy dime sized areola. Faint hairs she might think are abnormal so is frightened to have anyone see. No actual teats. She had all these, however, there are also breasts that shock a man with the sense that these are the first naked breasts he has seen in his life. She had those breasts as well.

The peach colored areola on her left side had one brail dot—by her twenties she might have a crop. It was her right areola though that transfixed him. It was a dainty volcano. What passed for her teat was a tiny raised ring with a crater. Ben realized the striations of her curious lips were mere hints. Her entire body was rich in attractions.

"Tell me," he said, "is there any way a customer might get to make out with one of the dancers? I would be more than happy to pay."

"Pay? No! Not someone handsome like you! Who's caught your eye?"

"Well, you have. I perhaps shouldn't say, but I haven't been able to stop thinking about you since we were playing last night. I could feel you weren't wearing anything under your nightie."

"I wish you had said. You've embarrassed me now."

Her face was so expressive, painted and close and Ben was just space junk sucked into its orbit.

"I'm the one who should be embarrassed. I'm turning into a stalker. I'm thinking about you so much I wouldn't care if I lost everything."

"You don't have to lose anything Daddy. We can do things. We just have to make them all part of a game."

"That would be my absolute dream."

"I'd like it too," she said.

"So this is the game where I've gone to a strip club and the girl there has agreed to make out?"

"I guess that's very unprofessional of me, but then I am only new," she said wide eyed with her pinkie finger raised to her lips.

At the risk of losing his load prematurely Ben moved his head into position to kiss her. "Come here then new girl."

It was certainly nicer kissing her half naked on a sofa than in her starchy school uniform on the hard floor. He undid his belt and guided her hand to his zip to undo it. Then he ventured to fondle her breasts.

She was pulling on the zip, but unsure where to stop. "Go on," he said. "There's no one around."

He found she enjoyed sucking kisses, with lips sealing and releasing but with mouths an inch open. The only air he was wanting was air coming out of her lungs. He had to have it all. But for their protection it all had to be role play.

"What's the game called," he whispered, "where you sleep in mom's bed and you and I pretend we are married?"

"Don't be silly. You know it. 'Mothers and fathers'."

"That's what we used to call it as well. Do they still pretend the mother and father are making a baby?"

"No, but we can play it that way if you like."

She was gangly and limp in his arms and almost too light. But for the narrowness of her waist, she wouldn't have had hips and her limbs and her neck belonged to a doll. If he looked too much he would balk at the prospect. But he couldn't do that. She would be offended to be dumped from her role as the mother.

He placed her on her feet, then, kneeling behind her, lowered her panties and helped her step through in her mother's high heels. His eyes followed her stockings to where they stopped on her thighs. You could kick a football between them. The smallest of her womanly contours were completely on show.

Ben realized he would have to fuck this one with the light on, on top of the covers, in front of the wardrobe door mirrors. There should be no running from the fact that such an underweight specimen under his body would be an aberrant spectacle.

He picked her back up in his arms. "Can I have a really close look at your baby bits, mommy?"

"If I can look at your daddy bits, sure."

He kissed her on the eye for her cute answer and said, "I'll have to lay you this way in that case. Hold your top leg up for me Kylie."

She had never been near her pubes with a razor, and might never need to, being naturally and virtually hairless. He should have known by her legs. No matter how long she went without shaving neither ever showed more than and handful of hairs and even then they were so faint that it was only in certain light you could see them.

Her hole looked as tight as it had felt on his finger that morning. And there he was accusing her of not eating those cucumbers! She would struggle inserting a bean.

From grating fresh truffle to full bodied wines, Ben had a thing for high class aromas. It was natural then for him to bury his nose in her folds. He breathed all the way out then deeply drew back on pure private schoolgirl. He could feel her exploring the head of his penis. He had to turn around to have a good look at this.

Few sights compare to a young face when she's giving you head. A cad would let go in her mouth. Maybe he was such a cad, but there were too many positions yet to enjoy.

With his legs together he took her under her armpits and dragged her vagina over his thighs, onto his shaft then slowly, slo-o-owly along it. He brought her to rest where the bundles of nerves in each of their organs would be as one bundle. With her weight in his hands he held her with her back arched and those inexorable breasts where he could best see them.

"You're utterly lovely you know."

"You're beautiful too."

Each of their hips were pulsating, like heart muscles compelled to serve life without their minds knowing.

"Don't forget, if we're being like this, you still should spend time with your sister."

"I know."

"And you know about telling your mother."

Of course she knew about telling her mother! The woman earned half a million a year. Everything depended on keeping her happy. Both Ben, and Kylie, would lose so many comforts if the status quo changed. Those now included the comforts they could receive from each other.

The first inch is the hardest and they were already there.

"Are you a virgin?"

"Ahu."

"I thought I could feel something. If you focus your mind on the kissing, and try not to think about what's happening down there, you might not even feel it when I go through."

That was just his hunch. Ben had never had the honor of an actual virgin. Ones he had known in his youth had frightened him off with the sense they would become too attached and demanding. That would never have been a problem if they were like Kylie. She could cling all she liked. She clung to him anyway. He clung to her. They were father and daughter. They clung. Incestuous relations might only last for a while. Their familial bond was forever.

That was enough over thinking the simple thing in his arms. All they were doing was playing a game, and many games can break a girl's hymen.

They were kissing, as before, but with more tongue and more more passion, until she moaned and he felt his cock plummet. He was profoundly inside her. He wanted this to be the way she would come, sucking on him from both ends, wanting his insides and him wanting hers.

Her sister was asleep. Her mother was away. It was Kylie's time to have him all to herself, for the kind of play time she needed now she was grown.

All he would do is stroke her skin with his hands, taking care to separate her buttocks with each upward pass and let air wash her freckle. Each pass was making her stiffen as if ready to come, so he let the next pass brush her sphincter. He was thinking how predictable it was that a posh private school girl would crave anal play, and what a shame it would be if she came before that had unfolded. He borrowed some lube from her cunt (no double dipping) to work his finger in circles, to the first knuckle.

That was enough. She was totally rigid. The only part moving was her actual asshole pulsating with her orgasm on the end of his finger. And all Ben had to do was let himself go so they could come together.

How exhausting! It took him a minute just to open his eyes. The first thing he saw was a light fitting, chosen by his wife, that he hated. A small sacrifice for this daughter.

Kylie was in her first year of college, studying to be a school teacher. She had figured it would not be so onerous a job as the one her mother had pursued. An easy job would give her more time at home with her father.

They had both just finished an exhaustive game of hide and seek with Natalie. Each saw playing with Natalie as the kid's reward for her unknowing role in their secret union. They gave her a solid hour's play time every night after dinner, playing whatever she wanted. Later most nights, even when her mom was at home, Kylie would sneak in to her dad to keep the game going. That night they would play the mature audiences version of hide and seek. She was trying to think of a hiding spot big enough to lay down in.

She never would go back to that internet forum. As much as she tried, she couldn't remember the site. That was a shame. Somewhere in the world were two anonymous, vicarious lurkers, who she would always want to thank for their coaching.

CPSIA information can be obtained
at www.ICGtesting.com
Printed in the USA
BVHW091218180321
602887BV00011B/1436